Tales of the Para-Imperium

Joel Kreissman

Copyright © 2019 Joel Kreissman

Cover art by Norman Rafferty

"Anthrophagy" originally published in *Seven Deadly Sins* by Thurston Howl, 2017

Fate™ is a trademark of Evil Hat Productions, LLC. The Powered by Fate logo is © Evil Hat Productions, LLC and is used with permission.

All Rights Reserved

ISBN: 9781794638457

CONTENTS

Contents

The Short Life of a Venusian Sky Pirate 6

Dandelion Seeds 10

A Brief History of the Federation: 27

The Federation of Parahuman Species: 31

The Final Battle: 36

Core World Planets and Cultures 42

Family Ties 47

Language: 58

Mercenaries: 59

Naming Conventions 62

Core Technology 65

Inside the Chinese Room 73

Religion: 86

For The Collective 90

History of The Kitsune 126

Sharing the Wealth: The Federation Economy in Detail 129

Spacer Survival Gear:	132
A World Lost:	134
The Parahuman Baseline:	144
Raising Capital:	147
The StarForge:	154
Some Outworlds of Note:	156
Utility Microbots: Elemental Technomagic	159
Anthropophagy	162
Unforeseen Dangers of Nanotech	169
"Marriage" in the Federation:	172
Beamferry:	175
FATE Core Setting:	176
About the Author:	186

The Short Life of a Venusian Sky Pirate

The alert went out, a freighter was sighted. The airborne pirate switched on a recording device as she changed into the pressure suit specifically designed for her chiropteran body. She would have preferred to fly in just the skin she was born with, but outside the pockets of breathable air around the aerostats it would be suicide. And the colonial authorities patrolled those pockets a bit too heavily for the rogues of Venusian society.

She flung herself across the vast open space that predominated the interior of their carrier airship, gliding to her fighter and diving in the cockpit. As she waited to be loaded into the ventral launch tube she donned her helmet, jacking a short cable on the interior into a port implanted in the back of her head, this cable was linked to a longer one connecting her helmet to the plane's systems. While physical controls remained the most effective means of piloting, the sensory input offered by a direct neural interface were unrivaled. When she was jacked in the craft felt like an extension of her body. She saw through cameras distributed all around the fuselage, she "heard" the plane's radar as if it were her own natural sonar, when the plane took a hit she felt, not pain exactly but she did receive a less incapacitating sensation that alerted her of damage.

After half a minute the robotic armature reached her plane and dropped it into the airlock at the end of the electromagnetic catapult. The hatch closed and the breathable air inside the compartment was exchanged for the toxic soup of Venus' atmosphere. Then the outer portal opened and the giant railgun threw her out at 5Gs. Turning on the electric props she swung the fightercraft towards their prey, a fat corporate cargo carrier transporting ore from one of the few surface bases to one of the wandering settlements far above the volcanic ground in the upper atmosphere. She briefly switched her attention back to the mothership she had just left, sleek and streamlined where their target was wide and bulky. She noted that the freighter was hanging almost a mile above their own airship, many of its compartments were probably filled with helium rather than nitro-oxy then, unmanned or minimal crew then, should be easy pickings.

The pirate squadron beelined for the cargo ship, as they approached the target's point defense cannons came online, she swerved, AI gunners still couldn't aim worth a damn unless it was travelling a straight line like a missile. She flicked on her guns, spitting a stream of lead at the enemy gun while staying out of its own line of fire. After a few seconds of fire it stopped shooting, good, she could unleash her missiles on the engines now. Except something fell out of the airship's lower cargo hatch, several small objects flared to life as rocket motors activated. Missiles? No, they were turning and pivoting to train their own guns on the pirate fighters, and now she could make out thin wings. Drones, remote piloted killer drones!

She was nearly out of bullets from the turret, and she wanted to save her missiles for the engines. As she tried to figure out what to do one of her wingmates exploded in a burst of shrapnel. She made a decision then and there and turned back towards the carrier, its guns could take out at least a few of the drones. As she flew back two of the drones followed, shooting at her as she fled. She felt a bullet pierce the skin of her left wing, now she didn't care about the cargo, if she didn't get out now she'd be dead. She punched a large red button on the control panel and the rocket in the back of her plane flared! See them try to catch her now.

But the drone pilots were prepared for that, each of the drones launched a small missile that locked onto the heat signature of her rocket. As the rocket burned through its fuel block she looked back and saw the missiles were gaining on her, in seconds they would overtake her. Frantically she grabbed the ejection lever and pulled hard, the canopy burst open and she was rocketed out as the missiles destroyed her fighter. The loss of her electronic senses disoriented her for a few seconds, but she was able to wrench the now useless jack out and fly away from her chair just in time. Trying to flap in a pressure suit was like trying to swim in a dress but she didn't have a choice. She headed to where she had seen the mothership last and was just in time to see a horrifying sight.

The two drones that had been following her began spinning in the air and dove straight into the pirate carrier's skin, firing their guns as they did so. The two drones tore gaping holes in the craft, and worse, she saw one exit through the far end. That would have torn through most of the compartments in the airship, most of her friends and crewmates would be dead now from the sulfuric acid or would die soon as the craft sank to the crushing depths below.

As she contemplated what to do next, if she was lucky she could make it to the cargo ship and try to surrender, a flap of the airship's torn skin hit her and she struggled to tear it off. When she finally managed to remove herself she found that she had already sunk several hundred feet, and even worse, in her efforts to free herself she had torn open the suit protecting one of her wings. As the acid burned the membranes she screamed in agony and continued to sink deeper and deeper. She fell silent just short of hitting the lava, cremating her remains in seconds.

Stream interrupted

Two technicians from the corporate ship watched the end of the stream they'd picked up from the pirate's suit camera. One of them shrugged and closed the window. "And that's it. I guess now the only question is whether we sell the video or upload it to the net."

"Well," said the other one, "on the one hand a video like this could get billions of views all over the solar system but not make us a micro. On the other flight schools would pay a lot to get this as a cautionary tale kind of thing."

"I suppose it would be more appropriate for her death to serve as a warning rather than entertainment." The first tech conceded. "We didn't get her name anywhere did we?"

"I didn't hear it." Replied the second. "Just as well, if she had some clan they might try to sue the company. As it is we'll have to edit out the destruction of the airship. And just what makes you think people won't watch it for fun?"

"Of course they will." The first technician stated. And commanded his implant to discreetly make a full copy of the video, unedited.

Dandelion Seeds

Hello, unknown listener, I am sure you are filled with curiosity about the outside universe, and I get the feeling that you would be more inclined to believe me if I were to indulge you.

My name is Jarlisse, and I might be the last of my kind.

First, you should probably know something about my "species", if we can be called such. I am what was called a "parahuman", an artificial mixture of my ancestral homeworld's single naturally evolved sapient race and the genetic material of one or more of the other, non-sapient species on said world. The first generation of parahumans were created by humans, the natural sapient species, as deep-space labor. Their governments afforded certain rights and protections to humans, but not to creatures that were quite clearly not human. So, some corporations found a loophole. They experimented with thousands of unique mixtures of human and animal genes and printed out the viable ones, then sent them out to the asteroids to bring back minerals.

However, the early parahumans shared the humans' drive for independence and soon the time came for them to rebel and claim the Asteroid Belt for their own. The parahumans, having no experience with self-governance, experimented with several different forms of government reasoning that with sufficient experimentation they'd be able to discern which ones worked out best and all would come to adopt the greatest government. But, as the humans had discovered years ago, it is very subjective which government is better and many parahumans could not bring themselves to agree on many ideas. And like humans, when parahumans disagreed on something strongly enough, there was the urge to settle the argument through violence.

The first major organized conflict between governments came from the Feudal Anarchy of Vesta and the Republic of Pallas. The Vestans believed that we should bioprint exact replicas of ourselves, with public safety and welfare entrusted to particular sets of replicas who had proven their ability and devotion to the cause. Whereas the Pallene released the genetic locks the humans placed on our "natural" reproductive systems that combined genes from two parahumans to produce a new one. Vesta saw Pallas as a threat to long-term stability and attempted to destroy them with nuclear explosives. Pallas retaliated in kind. They had been fighting for two Earth orbits when I was born to a Pallene couple. My mother was spliced with genes from what was called a "cheetah" while my father had "coyote" genetic material. All of us second-generation kids were bizarre mixes like that. Both habitats lost half their populations in that war, when it was realized how easily they could wipe each other out the two agreed to an alternative plan. They would instead devote their industries and destructive capabilities to designing and building ships that could plant colonies of their people on worlds around distant stars. Whoever colonized the most stars first won, I guess.

Pallas decided that, since even the fastest ship would take decades to reach any other star, they would train their children to crew the ships. Even the Grand Mayor zirself sent zir son and daughter into the program. I entered training when I was seven, I was barely half the size I am now. We were constantly tested to determine where to assign us, drilled on every possible emergency procedure they could imagine, trained to calculate orbital mechanics in our heads without mechanical assistance. At the age of ten, I was introduced to the rest of the crew I would serve with. Tony, the bear/tiger assigned to engineering. Rachel, rabbit/mouse pilot. Stewart, the musteline biologist. And myself, the cheeyote communications tech. We would carry a payload comprising all the equipment to build a self-sufficient colony on a distant planet. Hydroponics beds, pre-fabbed shelters, mining drones, omni-printers to make whatever non-living items or structures we needed. We also brought bioprinters to make food and the colonists themselves. There were thousands of gamete samples preserved in cryogenic storage in the hold, we could mix them up however we wished for maximum genetic diversity and print them into a new colonist who would be rapid-trained like the corporations used to do. But as soon as the colony was sustainable we would allow the colonists to breed naturally. We were expected to pair up with crewmates, or possibly any colonists who caught our eye, and make babies ourselves once the mission was complete. But no sooner, we couldn't afford to waste time raising kids while running a starship. So, when we turned fourteen gamete samples from each one of us were taken and placed into storage, and our plumbing was surgically modified so that those samples were the only way we could ever reproduce. Our ship was ready for departure to the star system designated "Epsilon Indi" a couple years after that.

I remember watching my parents wave goodbye over the monitor that displayed a video stream transmitted by radio from the Pallas habitat as the nuclear fusion propulsion system kicked in. I think back to that moment now and have to remind myself that whatever radio waves brought the doom upon us all were transmitted long before that fateful day.

Over the next six years we fell into a comfortable routine of maintenance checks, course corrections, and consumption of assorted forms of entertainment. Mostly stored in the libraries of the ship's computer but we did get the occasional data packet from Pallas, or tried to write our own material. The memory of Stewart's weekly poetry readings still makes me gag. We also found other, non-written ways to entertain ourselves in each other, if you know what I mean. Tony was always so strong and controlling, Stewart, rather flexible if you know what I mean, while Rachel could do surprising things with those grass-clipping teeth of hers.

All this while, I was assigned to keep vigilant watch on any and all communications from home. However, after a couple years it got boring just sitting by the comm station and replying "confirmed" to every message so I set a program to respond automatically and alert my handheld comm whenever someone called. Messages were coming less and less frequently as time went by anyways.

Then, one day, it all changed.

We hadn't received any messages in three months. To be honest, it took them more than seven months to reach us by that point in our journey and an equal amount of time to get back home so the delay was understandable. We thought nothing of the long delay until one day when we received a report that chilled us to the very bones.

"Earth has been attacked." The simple text message started. "An object massing approximately ten million metric tonnes and traveling at 90% of the speed of light collided with the planet from somewhere far outside the solar system. Nothing on the surface survived, the crust was split and the mantle exposed." It ended with a line that tore at the very foundations of our belief system. "Scientific consensus is near unanimous. It could not have been natural and it cannot be the result of any action by human or parahuman technology. We are at war with an alien civilization."

Needless to say we were dumbfounded. Alien civilization? That was the stuff of old science-fiction. The humans had concluded long ago that they were the only intelligent life in the known universe, and even after creating us we weren't very alien. We just sat there in the media room staring at the last sentence in shock until finally one of us gathered themself up enough to speak.

"They're doomed." Tony said simply. "Nothing they can do."

Stewart disagreed to an extent. "They can hide. The aliens have only attacked Earth. It said nothing about the Asteroids or Mars domes or the Venus aerostats. If they dampen their emissions to background levels they might avoid detection and escape further attacks."

"Dampening emissions sounds like something we could do." Rachel cut in. "I could shut off the active sensors, rely on passive only. Maybe even cut the drive to minimal pulse. But that would vastly extend our travel time to Epsilon Indi."

I asked her, "How much longer?"

The bunnymouse sighed. "Eighty years, give or take." She leaned forward on the table and groaned. "We might not live that long."

Humans can live about a hundred years, given proper care is taken. On the other hand no one knew how long parahumans could live, the oldest of us would only be in their fifties by now. Still, we were already twenty. The odds of us living through another eight decades seemed slim.

Stewart, of course, had worked out another answer. "We have the life support capacity to sustain three times our number, indefinitely. We could, you know..."

I looked up. "Lay our hopes and dreams on the next generation?"

The weasel mix grinned. "You were always a better poet than I."

Tony the bear-tiger snarled to bring the meeting to order. "We still need to figure out how to avoid the same fate as Earth." He said. "Have you sent a reply?" He directed straight at me.

"No, I..." I stopped. The machine would have sent a reply automatically upon receipt of the message. Just a brief confirmation code but it would still be a traceable signal. "I need to go change some settings." I rushed off before any of them could ask me what was wrong.

That night I spent in Tony's cabin, his body substituting for a blanket. I felt so vulnerable, so scared of what might happen next, and his pseudo-ursine arms felt safe and secure. No matter how little they might actually defend against that which now threatened us.

Some time after we'd finished our love-making I found myself muttering "I doomed us." As I lay there under Tony. At the sound of my voice he snorted awake and looked at me quizzically. I adjusted my position to look him directly in the eyes and elaborated. "I set up an automated response to Earth years ago. We sent back a message that will lead the aliens straight to us."

He paused for a minute, trying to formulate his response in a way that wouldn't make me even more upset. "Lisa," he said, for that was how we liked to shorten my name. "That message was on a tight-beam, correct? Going only to Pallas?"

"Yes." I confirmed, feeling maybe the faintest hints of relief. "But what if they attack Pallas and set up a listening station there before the message reaches Sol? Then we're done for."

He chuckled as if he were one of our instructors back in training and I had just asked a silly question. "I very much doubt that." The tiger-bear said. "It will take less than a year for our message to reach home. Their use of a relativistic "sniper" shot from outside our detection range indicates that they didn't want to risk a full-out confrontation with Earth so any invasion force would be at least a light-year out. Nothing capable of thinking, or even computation, could survive the acceleration needed to get a ship that far away to Sol before the message arrived."

Tony seemed to be making sense, I wasn't an engineer like him or an astronavigator like Rachel, but I knew the detection range of a starship-sized object using Earth's telescopes. It was, in fact, over 1.1 light-years. But, something that had long been dismissed as fantastical rose to the front of my thoughts. "What if they have faster-than-light drive?"

Tony actually laughed out loud at that. "Don't be ridiculous." He exclaimed. "Not only is that impossible, but on the long chance that they did have FTL they wouldn't have bothered accelerating that giant rock up to .9c. They could have just "warped in" a bunch of nukes near all our major population centers." He waved a hand idly as he spoke. "It costs so much energy to accelerate something that large to that speed and it is detectable from so far away that they wouldn't have bothered if they could bypass the speed of light barrier."

I finally was able to relax then. If he was so sure that we were safe, then it was so. It could be no other way. I drew my arms out from under Tony and wrapped them around his thick chest. "I definitely want your children." I told him.

He laughed again. "What? Going to leave poor Rachel stuck with Stewart?"

"Oh, you know him. He'll probably insist that we 'mix-and-match' mates for maximum genetic diversity or something like that." There would be time to work out the details of who would be having whose kids later, we had nothing but time to waste now.

For four years we heard nothing else from home. We kept on going almost mechanically. Throwing ourselves into our work to distract ourselves from the literal world-shattering revelations. In every moment of idleness our minds crept back to thoughts of habitat domes exploding under a rain of alien fire. We ran through the entertainment library's collection of any and all media that didn't involve alien invasions and strained the synthesizer's ability to produce stimulants to keep us from sleeping, and dreaming, as little as possible.

When we couldn't avoid it and had to sleep we dreamed horrible dreams of the worst things our subconscious could invent. Spidery walkers multiple stories high striding through habitat domes stomping on pedestrians. Swarms of glistening grey assemblers turning people into rubbery monsters with too many tentacles and feelers (if any octopi are listening, no offense), and worst of all: unseen snipers launching planetoids at Pallas, shattering it into a million shards of rock and dust without ever revealing themselves.

Finally, we heard something back from Sol system. Unlike the tight-beams sent from Pallas, this was a broad-spectrum transmission sent in all directions at once. I still have a recording, I might as well re-transmit it now, even though you've probably heard it already.

"This is an automated beacon broadcasting what may well be the last message ever sent by the human race. Five years ago, our homeworld, Earth was struck by a moon-sized projectile travelling at 90% of the speed of light. The debris took out most of our habitats in Earth's orbit, a few million of us survived elsewhere in the solar system. Then the rest of the invasion force arrived. Machines, vast machines kilometers in length that home in on any sources of radio transmissions, and annihilate them. We pray they are not intelligent and are simply weapons fired by a xenophobic alien race. But they've almost completed their work, we estimate that there's only a couple hundred of us left in the system. We're sending this message in hopes that there is someone out there who can hear it and beware. This universe is more hostile than we thought. They attack radio transmitters, dismantle whatever devices you are using to listen to this before they find you."

Stewart broke down halfway through the message, collapsing into a sobbing, blubbering heap, while Rachel made it to the last sentence before joining him on the floor. Me and Tony just barely managed to hold on. The entire Sol system demolished? All of humanity and parahumanity dead save for us few individuals out in deep space? It was almost too much to grasp.

The big tiger-bear held me close in his strong embrace. I will always remember how tightly and warmly he held me. How he reassured me "we're still here, we're still here." As if merely remaining alive was reason for hope. But something nagged at me, the final message had said five years ago when we were notified of the destruction of Earth four years ago. They'd waited most of a year before informing us that 99.9999% of all known sapient life in the universe were dead. The difference in transmission distance between then and now was barely a light-month or two. And they had not even sent us any updates on how the war was going until it was all but over. Not to mention that the final message was a broad-range burst rather than concentrated in any way. Had the Pallas long-range radio array been one of the first targets after Earth? It made sense given how it was a giant transmitter and the machines were said to home in on radio signals. Had Pallas itself been destroyed so early in the conflict?

I decided that if Pallas had been destroyed quickly, then they were the lucky ones. The survivors would have had to run and hide somewhere deep in the asteroids or near the gas giants or somewhere. Always on the move, living in terror of some unseen enemy finding them and wiping them out from millions of kilometers away. Just waiting out here for news for that long had been horrible. Imagine knowing what was going on, knowing you could not outrun them, and not knowing when you would be found. I could not think of a worse way to live.

Slowly, Tony loosened the grip of his heavy, fur-covered arms and I slumped out of their grasp into a chair. I watched as he strode over to comfort Rachel and Stewart, admiring his mental fortitude as well as his physical strength. It's why what happened next shocked me so much.

Barely two weeks after the fateful message Tony told us that the main engine had some sort of issue and he would need to go outside to repair it. We all waved him good luck as he donned his vacuum suit and strode out the airlock to climb along the exterior of the craft towards the rear. We watched on the cameras as he did something out there, but so far as we could tell he was just disassembling and reassembling the same component over and over again, it was puzzling to be honest.

Then something on Rachel's personal comm unit chimed and her face fell. "What is it?" I asked, thinking that the worst was happening.

She tapped her unit a few times on the touch-screen, breathing rapidly as she tried to find what she was looking for. Then calmed down a little. "It's okay." She said. "The system was set to detonate the next charge in a few minutes, but Tony said the launcher wasn't operational and the charges have safeties preventing them from detonating until they're a safe distance away."

Our ship was propelled by a massive load of nuclear fusion explosives. We called it the "Daedalus Drive" after a myth about an ancient inventor who figured out how to fly and flew so close to the sun he got burnt. I guess they had a sense of irony. Every so often the ship would chuck one out behind us and detonate it. A miniature sun appearing for an instant to shove us a little closer to our destination. Tony was working on the machine that threw those bombs out behind us now. "Maybe you should cancel it anyways." I suggested. "Wouldn't want to put any undue strain on the systems."

"Good idea." The rabbit-mouse admitted, and opened another page and quickly tapped out a sequence of keys. And tapped those keys again. And a third time. "What the hell is going on?" She exclaimed. "My password isn't working."

"What do you mean it's not working?" Stewart asked. "The only other one with access to the engine controls is out there working on it." Then the weasel's eyes grew very wide all of a sudden. "Wait, can you check on the status of that thing he's trying to fix?"

"Easily." Rachel said. "Why would you..." She stared at the readout on her device. "Oh no."

"What's going on?" I exclaimed.

"The launcher is operational." She replied. "It's been operational the whole time. It's going to launch, and detonate!"

I scrambled to my communications console. Most of the surfaces were covered in dust from disuse but I was still able to activate the short-range radio. It would dissipate into incomprehensible static within light-hours but Tony's suit would be able to pick it up easily. I flicked on the microphone and spoke slowly but worriedly into it. "Tony. The launcher is operational. I repeat, the launcher is operational, come back in." No response. "Tony, a bomb is about to be launched, please get in here before it blows." Still nothing, had he disabled his radio? "Tony! Please, get in here!" I yelled into the mic but still he did nothing.

Stewart started to suit up to go out and grab him the hard way, but it was too late. The external cams registered the launch tube opening and a silvery spherical object exiting, then the cameras switched off to protect our vision from the light. In less than a minute the cameras reactivated, there was no trace of Tony to be seen, nothing but the frayed end of a tether whipping back to wrap itself around the ship. He was gone.

Ten minutes later we were all in the recreation room drinking large mugs of relaxant tea and trying to collect our nerves enough to speak. Rachel was the first.

"He must have known." She said, almost robotically, before taking another sip of her beverage. "He must have planned it out, there's no way he could have been mistaken about the launcher."

"You think he wanted to end it all?" Stewart asked, his hands trembling as he gripped his mug in both of them.

"He wouldn't have." I insisted flatly. "He was too strong. He wouldn't have done something so weak."

Stewart sighed and set down his drink. "It's not a simple case of 'weakness vs. strength'." He said. "I studied something about human psychology during training. It said that people who entertain thoughts of suicide aren't afraid, or cowardly, or anything like that. They can't imagine themselves ever being happy. They have no hope, no reason to remain alive."

"That still doesn't sound like him." I said.

Rachel interjected with a suggestion of her own. "Maybe we should check out his room. There might be something in there we never knew about." We agreed. We emptied our mugs and set out for his cabin out in the rear wheel.

Our ship has its living spaces in two wheels that spin in order to simulate gravity using centrifugal force. The smaller rear wheel actually consists of four unconnected sections on the ends of long "spokes" that hold our personal cabins. The isolation ensures that if one cabin is opened to space the others won't be so easily affected, and discourages rooming together as the area is cramped. Tony's room was as sparsely adorned as the rest of ours, having been taught from a young age not to clutter up our scarce living space with useless ornaments. There was a bunk recessed into the wall on one side, and a standing desk on the other with a large-screened computer terminal and a couple print books. Backup repair manuals in case the power went out.

While Stewart and Rachel searched the bed I picked up one of the books, a user's guide to the radioisotope thermoelectric generator that provided us with power. It seemed strange to me, a race that had been raised from the start on e-tablets using something so primitive as "paper" to store information. I flicked through a few chapters, it was full of complex diagrams and language I couldn't have hoped to understand. But I noticed that the top corner of one page in the middle had been folded over, as I opened the book to that specific page to inspect it I found a single large word written by hand across the page. "Dandelion".

I showed it to the others and Rachel entered the word into the password prompt on her personal unit. It worked. And not only did she once again have manual control of the ship's drive system, but there was a message there, waiting for her. She opened it as we glanced over her shoulder.

The message contained an image file of the stars behind us, with one point in particular highlighted. Annotations listed the spectral analysis of the point's light, there was something about "antimatter?", and the velocity and direction of the object. It was headed straight for us, traveling at almost a quarter of the speed of light, but it was decelerating, rapidly. The aliens had found us.

"What are we going to do?" Rachel asked me, her voice quavering.

"I..." I trailed off as I flipped more frantically through the book. There were more notes, scattered hypotheses. Some suggested that the other ships had used the big rock as a distraction and slipped in at their leisure. Or they were coasting in already when the rock had been launched. Even a brief suggestion that maybe they did have FTL after all. "I don't know."

More than the destruction of Earth, more than the razing of the Solar System, more than Tony's death, the news that we had been found shook us. Tony's data indicated that we had three months before it reached us. Our first impulse was to abandon all pretenses of concealment and go at full throttle, since we had already been found. Rachel set the launcher to throw out nukes every 15 minutes, any faster and the drive plate would not be able to dissipate the heat and melt. Without the plate protecting the ship the rear of the craft would melt or be outright vaporized. As that section contained our main drive section, our power generator, and the life support scrubbers we would be dead in space if it were destroyed.

Our pursuer accelerated. Our effort had given us no more than two more weeks.

We didn't want to talk about it. The only way we felt we could cope was to throw ourselves into our work with even more fervor than before. And to occupy any spare time studying to fill Tony's duties. Even if we weren't on such a short deadline there wouldn't have been a reason to bioprint a full-time replacement for him. We had basic training in each other's duties and it was unlikely we'd have a major issue in that area in the time we had left.

We largely avoided one another for the next week. We didn't want to talk about what had happened. Rachel spent almost all her time at the bridge, leaving me and Stewart to bounce around the ship between our original jobs and Tony's vacated duties. Even then, we barely spoke, we just glided past each other, him simply mumbling "dandelion seeds" under his breath.

I shouldn't have been surprised at what happened next. He didn't even try explaining his actions, we couldn't find any hints in his cabin or his lab. All we knew was neither me nor Rachel saw Stewart for a couple days and we didn't think anything of it until I checked on the life-support logs and noticed that O2 recycling had diminished by a third in the past couple days. I couldn't find any mechanical problems that could account for the change, and I didn't feel any faintness or shortness of breath so I decided to seek out Stewart for his advice.

    I couldn't find him in the Bio lab, or the Rec room, or his cabin, or in Tony's room. Finally I went over to the bridge to ask Rachel if she had seen him anywhere. She was hanging suspended in the middle of the gravity-less compartment staring blankly into open space through the main screen covering most of the far wall of the bridge. I cleared my throat loudly to draw her attention and the mouse-rabbit turned to face me. Giving me a serious look of annoyance as I disturbed her reverie.

    "Sorry," I apologized quickly, "but I was just wondering if you had seen Stewart today."

    "No," she replied dismissively, "have you checked his cabin?"

    "I have," I replied coolly, "and all the other cabins and compartments."

    Her ears drooped and her eyes widened in shock. "You checked the entire ship and couldn't find him anywhere?" She exclaimed in disturbed surprise. "I'll pull up all the camera feeds now."

    The stars on the main screen shrunk to one corner, with the rest of the giant monitor now occupied by the feeds from the various security cameras scattered throughout the craft. There was one in each cabin, pointed away from the bed so that one couldn't peep in on anyone sleeping, but I had already checked all the bunks. Each of the larger compartments, including the bridge, had two cameras facing in opposite directions so as to cover the entire room. The central shaft had cameras every five feet and the fore and aft airlocks each had one camera. The exterior had four at each end of the long ship for observing crew performing extravehicular activities, like those we had used to watch Tony die. About twenty-nine security cameras in total, thirty sections to the monitor counting the navigation feed. None of the live feeds showed any trace of Stewart, where could he be?

    Then Rachel asked me when I'd last seen Stewart. I couldn't remember, but recalling the life support data, I told her it was three days ago. She called up recordings from that day. We saw Stewart wake up, dress, eat breakfast, brush his teeth, and go in to the lab. Zipping forward at several times faster than normal play speed we saw him take out a sample cuvette with a sample of gametes for the colony we were intended to start, consider it for several minutes, then place it and several other cuvettes in a bag and carry the bag out to the aft airlock. We watched in horror as he carelessly shook the bag out into the airlock, then came back through the interior door and grabbed more and more loads of gametes, releasing them all out into the airlock space. Then, eventually, he gathered up all the cuvettes in the airlock in one large armful, mouthed two words directly at the airlock camera, and opened the outer door.

We gasped in shock as he opened the door, letting the air rush out. He remained inside for a few more moments, as there was not nearly enough air pressure to push him out. Then he positioned himself against the inner door, coiled, and leaped out into open space. Carrying the gametes with him.

Parahumans were designed to live in space. The first generation had titanium-plated bones to prevent loss of strength from microgravity-induced osteoporosis. As we of the second generation grew in wombs instead of being bioprinted with fully adult bodies we lacked those bones and needed to spend much of our time in centrifuges, but we still retained our parents' enhanced oxygen retention. Our blood and muscles were so filled with hemoglobin and myoglobin as to be almost black in color. We could remain conscious in an environment completely devoid of oxygen for ten minutes and alive for an hour. But Stewart had left the ship more than two days ago without any sort of reserve oxygen supply or anything. It was impossible for him to still be alive at this point.

We watched, helplessly, as the external cameras tracked his flailing body careening out into open space. His arms kept alternately folding and flicking out, as if he were throwing things. We were puzzled as to what he was doing until the light from a detonation flashed off a small glass tube leaving his hand. He was throwing the samples in all directions. We watched in frozen horror until he was so far away as to be invisible to the naked eye.

Then Rachel asked me if I had checked on gamete storage since the weasel's disappearance. I turned and ran, bouncing off the walls in the microgravity, until I had reached the spoke leading to the bio lab. The freezer had closed automatically, and I had to undo all the assorted locks to open it and check the contents.

It was empty. The whole compartment had been cleaned out. He had even taken our own potential babies. A colony was no longer possible.

I didn't return to work after that. I just went back to my cabin, turned out the lights, and curled up in my bed. For the first time in months I let myself think. Really think hard. I wondered, perhaps me and Rachel could clone ourselves when we reached the planet. The bioprinter was still intact, and even if our gonads were gone our every cell contained a full genome. I could study how to perform the biologist's duties and replicate samples of our cells into the stem cells used by the bioprinter to fabricate new parahumans. There wouldn't be much genetic diversity in the new colony, even if we found some skin or hair cells from Tony or Stewart and the clones were allowed to breed naturally. They'd be inbreeding within three generations.

But, we could just keep on cloning, so long as we kept the machines working. Heck, we could even pull it off with a single genetic template maybe. There was no need for both of us to survive.

Then it hit me. There was no way that someone as strong as Tony would commit suicide, and it was Rachel who told me that the launcher was working after all. And now it was down to just me and her. Would I be the next one to "kill herself"? Would Rachel continue on to Epsilon Indi to rule over a new planet full of copies of herself? She may have even faked the transmissions from Sol, she knew enough about radio to pull it off, somehow.

It was so clear to me now, one of us had to die soon, and I didn't intend it to be me. I would have to kill her before she killed me. And I wouldn't bother making it look like a suicide, there was no one left to object. It wasn't even really murder, when you thought about it, it was self-defense.

There weren't any obvious weapons like guns or knives on board. Barely even any eating utensils as we just ate with our hands or sipped it out of the container. But there were some power tools in the engineering section, and Rachel had neglected to remove them. I dismissed a circular saw and a plasma cutter as too heavy and bulky to wield as effective weapons, they were probably designed that way. But I found a cordless drill and the largest, sharpest bit in the inventory, I'd just need to press it against her in the right spot and start drilling. I took the drill and sprang forth towards the bridge with death on my mind.

The mouse-rabbit was in the same fugue-like state she was in when I'd come to talk to her about Stewart. Soundlessly, I pushed off towards her with one hand outstretched to grab her protruding ears and the other one holding the drill ready. Somehow, she heard me and turned slightly to look at me. Seeing the drill she scrambled frantically to grab something for mobility while yelling "Lisa, what are you doing?"

I got hold of her leg as it waved near me. She jackknifed back and caught hold of a console, whipping me towards a wall. I shoved the drill point-first into her other leg and used it as leverage to swing my free hand further up to her torso, where I grabbed her at the shoulder.

She screamed in pain as the drill punctured her leg, black droplets of blood streamed out as I removed it and swung it up towards her head. "Why are you doing this?" She begged as I brought the drill up against her eye.

I didn't give her the satisfaction of my reply. I pressed the trigger of the drill and the bit began spinning and whirring loudly as I thrust it towards her. She swung her head to the side and I only grazed her on the first pass, so I took hold of her head in my free hand and adjusted my angle so that it bored into the side of her cranium. Rachel bit down on my hand with those long rodent incisors of hers, but my drill was already tearing chunks out of her brain and in seconds her body went limp.

I let go and cast aside the corpse, the drill bit still in her head. I had won, I thought, I had survived. Now, I would need to figure out how to clone myself so as to fill all the empty crew positions and soon. Maybe I could find enough DNA traces of Tony and Stewart to clone them, and then I could print off some new ovaries for myself and bear their children. But I certainly wouldn't be cloning this psychopathic bitch who had murdered them, her genes would be flushed out into the void never to live again.

But, doubt struck me and Rachel's body turned to face me, her blank eyes staring past me and seeing nothing ever again. What if I'd made a mistake? What if the monsters were real? It was ridiculous but that small part of my brain would not let the idea go so I went back to the telescope controls and calibrated them to find the so-called pursuer that Tony had supposedly detected.

It was there, and it was getting closer.

I kept Rachel's body with me for the next week. I couldn't bring myself to dispose of her like some piece of garbage now that I knew I'd murdered her for no good reason. I covered the hole in her head with a bandage and placed her on her barely used bed, which I came by to visit every day before going to work. One day I found myself getting into bed next to her and snuggling up to her corpse like it was a large stuffed animal, but I had to rinse off the fluids that were leaking out as she decayed the following morning. The deterioration reminded me that she couldn't stay there, it would stink up the entire ship and spread bacteria all over. Reluctantly, I decided to take her out the airlock after that moment of weakness.

I didn't bother with a space suit, I wouldn't be out long, as I carried her carcass out into the aft lock. I closed the inner door behind me and triggered the decompression cycle. My eardrums popped and I got a headache from the sinus pressure as the air was sucked out, but I held on and kept going. I opened the outer door and looked out into the depths of space. Inky blackness, with only a few distant pinpricks of light for illumination, it seemed to call to me as I stood there on the threshold to oblivion. I pulled Rachel out to the edge of the doorway and straightened her out to throw her away. I gave her one last look into those glassy eyes and mouthed the word "goodbye" before gently pushing her out into space.

I considered leaping out to join her, but I couldn't, something was still holding me back. I watched her float away into the endless night until my vision began to swim from lack of oxygen, then I finally closed the outer door and started the compression cycle just before I lost consciousness.

I dreamt fitfully as I lay there in the airlock, my brain acting up as it slowly regained enough air to function. I found myself kneeling in a dark room before a trio of podiums where my dead friends stood. They accused me of killing them, not by drilling a hole in Rachel's skull, but by leading the Destroyer to the ship with my automated messages. I tried to explain that with the time delay it could have been any of the messages sent out before I received the notification of the Earth's demise but they kept shouting me down.

I woke after too long a period of unconsciousness in the airlock. I scrambled to the inner door and glided back in, shutting it with a start. My friends would be back the next time I slept, I just knew it, would they be there waiting for me if I killed myself now? Maybe if I made an effort to ensure their deaths meant something they might leave me alone.

That was when I started recording these messages. It's been two weeks since I started telling my story to the stars. In that time I have slept six times and contemplated suicide twice as often. They visit me in my dreams again and again, always telling me that "I haven't paid yet". What else can I do?

The Destroyer creeps ever closer. Two and a half months before it catches up with me. Unless its weapons have extremely long range like what they used to destroy Earth. The computers are set to transmit the message the instant they detect anything approaching within a light-minute of the ship.

Six weeks before its scheduled to reach me and the Destroyer is just entering visual range. It's... huge. My ship is bigger than any skyscraper ever built on Earth and this thing looks like it could swallow me up and have room for the rest of the colony fleet. I can't really make out much more detail, it seems like just a massive block of metal with a constant nuclear flare at the far end. How could it store so much fuel? What does it use for fuel?

My friends haven't let up on their nocturnal haunting. Stewart's shade has taken to mumbling that one phrase he kept repeating in the week before he jumped out into eternity. "Dandelion seeds." I couldn't imagine what it could mean until I remembered that Tony's new password was "dandelion", I looked it up in the encyclopedia. Dandelions were a kind of flowering plant native to Earth that were considered a weed by most cultures. The leaves were covered in spines but the little yellow flowers looked kind of pretty. However, it was their lifecycle that fascinated Tony and Stewart. The flowers closed after a day or two, then in their place grew a sphere of seeds with white wisp-like parachutes. The wind blew on the seeds and they'd be carried away to land in distant field and grow until some gardener found and uprooted them. Over a hundred seeds per plant, only a small fraction of them would take root and an even smaller percentage would have the opportunity to produce their own seeds.

Was that what Stewart was thinking when he threw the gamete samples into space? It makes no sense, he must have known they'd never grow without a uterus or bioprinter to sustain them.

Oh well, I suppose the strain must have gotten to him. Like it did to me.

I'm so sorry Rachel. I wish you were still here to keep my mind off the inevitable.

Three weeks left and now the Destroyer is clearer in my view. It appears to be unfolding somehow. The front end is separating into eight long sections that are spreading out like arms. Does it mean to grab me?

Why doesn't it just shoot me and get it over with?

Less than a week left and I can see the spaces between the arms filling with some kind of foamy substance. Radar pings indicate that it's soft, but very strong and dense. It may somehow even be capable of stopping and securing an object traveling as fast as myself.

Does it want to study me? That makes no sense. If they wanted to dissect parahumans or put them into a zoo they would have had plenty of opportunity when they were burning the Sol system to the ground years ago. Analyze the computer banks for information? Everything there is public domain, it would have been in the system-wide internet when they got to...

Oh shit, they're after the coordinates to the other colony expeditions. Only the ships and mission control back on Pallas would have known the exact trajectories and destinations of each craft. Mission control would no doubt have erased the servers, even vaporized them, as soon as Earth was destroyed. So I might be their only way to discover where the other remnants of parahumanity have hidden themselves.

I need to stop talking and wipe the databanks.

I may have wiped the servers but they could probably reconstruct the data from the molecular traces on the solid-state cards. I would need to vaporize the very same computers that the ship requires to stay functional.

I've given Tony's words some more thought. Those samples weren't the dandelion seeds he was talking about. We, the entire ship and its crew, were just one seed. A seed ship, a shot in the dark, a long chance. So long as one seed ship plants a colony and develops enough to build its own seed ships the parahuman race survives. If one or two never make it to their destinations it doesn't matter.

And we were just a failed seed. I can die, knowing that my civilization can continue without me. With this final act to ensure that my friends may even forgive me and let me rest in peace.

That is why I'm sending this warning. If you're hearing this, your civilization is in grave danger. You can detect long-wave radio, so I'm assuming that either you have already developed the technology to generate radio waves, or you will soon. If you've just started producing radio, then congratulations, you have maybe 10 generations left if my people are any indication. I don't know if you're human, parahuman, or some bug-eyed alien race we never had the chance to make contact with. But no matter what you look like my advice is the same.

Shut off your radios and get working on escaping your solar system. Fast.

If the machine pursuing me can capture a vessel traveling at my speed I can't do anything to harm it. Not even if I detonated every propulsion nuke on board simultaneously. But I could easily reduce this ship to its base atoms.

Static

This has been a recording from the archives of the New Alexandria Library, Secland capital arcology, Alpha Centauri A, the Interstellar Federation of Parahuman Species.

A Brief History of the Federation:

After three interplanetary wars the Pallas republic decided that it was time to start looking again for a new home. This time one that would be even more inaccessible. After much research it was found that a small craft propelled by several hundred tons of thermonuclear explosives could carry a skeleton crew with a load of frozen embryos, and the new fabrication swarms would make it fairly simple to construct these craft. They sent out half a dozen ships before the Calamity, and many other planetoids and even the planets of Earth and Mars followed suit. But before the first colony ship was halfway to its destination the Sol system suddenly went dark, the crews of these miniscule lifeboats waited, terrified, to find out what the reason was. Eventually they got their answer.
"This is an automated beacon broadcasting what may well be the last message ever sent by the human race. Five years ago, our homeworld, Earth was struck by a 50-ton projectile travelling at 90% of the speed of light. The debris took out most of our habitats in Earth's orbit, a few million of us survived elsewhere in the solar system. Then the rest of the invasion force arrived. Machines, vast machines kilometers in length that home in on any sources of radio transmissions, and annihilate them. We pray they are not intelligent and are simply weapons fired by a xenophobic alien race. But they've almost completed their work, we estimate that there's only a couple hundred of us left in the system. We're sending this message in hopes that there is someone out there who

can hear it and beware. This universe is more hostile than we thought. They attack radio transmitters, dismantle whatever devices you are listening to this on before they find you."

The message, broadcast on the longest-wave radio known to man and paraman, repeated for three weeks before it cut out. Most of the colonists despaired at this news, as far as they knew they in their little ship were the last remnant of Earth, an untold number could not take the strain and destroyed themselves and their ship. Others decided to take the message's advice and go dark, some taking it so far as to make pacts to abandon all technology as soon as they reached an inhabitable planet. Alpha Centauri, the closest star system to Sol, was settled by three different ships on the same nearly Earthlike planet. Second Landing, or SecLand as the planet came to be known, was first colonized by a small group of Pallene Parahumans who claimed the entire planet in the name of the great (presumed deceased) leader Argentum. To honor zim, they bioprinted a first generation of 500 genetically distinct and very fertile Parahumans from the assorted sperm and eggs donated by exuberant citizens. Including a male and female grown from Argentum's own genome spliced with traces of zir companions and advisors. This pair entered politics and quickly usurped the founders as the grand mayor of the colony. By the time the second ship arrived the planet had a population of 2,000 and had a burgeoning industrial base. This ship and the others that followed were integrated into the new republic.

As the centuries passed, colonies began experimenting with alternative means of communicating long distances. Planetside populations favored heavy use of fibre optics, while those who maintained spacecraft and asteroid colonies generally preferred tight-beam laser transceivers.

Eventually scientists on SecLand made two breakthroughs in the field of quantum mechanics. The first was the discovery that entangled particles exist everywhere in the universe, scattered throughout eternity, and that some of the particles that make up sentient beings' nervous systems are entangled with those of other sentients, in particular identical twins. With training these twins could be made to communicate with each other by words or feelings or in rare cases images, which they could relay to others. Unfortunately this resolution was low and telepaths with cranial implants seemed to have the weakest connections. But it did lead to the second innovation, comm units that contained entangled particles enabling them to send data up to and including video that could be exported off unit. Unfortunately these entangled particles were expensive, to the tune of 10,000 credits for a kilobyte's worth, and each bit severed the connection between a pair.

This was enough though, to justify the deployment of probes to the other known colonies fitted with the new QE comms. This enabled regular communication between the governments of these systems, once any initial suspicion had been overcome. However, bandwidth was in too short supply for any useful data transfer, the various systems had been isolated from one another for over a millennium at this point and had diverged massively. There was a wealth of information out there just waiting for someone to grasp it. Eventually a consortium called Interstellar Expeditions was founded with the objective of combining the old rapid construction techs with new matter annihilation to build "data freighters" that would go out into the black carrying research journals, works of fiction, and other information that could be of value to distant suns and bring back data that would be just as valuable to SecLand. The first expedition took fifty Terran years to return but the crew was able to buy their ship outright and went back out. Others followed suit, and still other smaller groups got similar ideas, the consortium didn't last long but the investors at least got rich off it.

Five more centuries passed, more systems were contacted, some were found burned and shattered like Sol. But eventually, physicists on SecLand made another breakthrough. With access to astronomical data and the works of physicists from over a dozen systems they were finally able to develop a means of producing a transversable wormhole. The two mouths of the wormhole had to be transported to the two destinations to be connected, at under 25% light speed no less, but once they were in place they were held open by exotic matter and could move traffic and information between star systems in hours rather than years. When the first stargate, between Alpha Centauri and Tau Ceti, was laid down grand mayor Selkd the Uniter, a descendant of Argentum's bioprinted progeny, pushed for a unification of all Parahuman worlds under a single Federation that would prevent yet another Calamity from happening. The Church of the Noosphere, up until then a minor sect in the Centauri system, declared their unilateral support for Selkd and proclaimed that the noospheres of Centauri and Ceti would soon become one. The government of Tau Ceti agreed, followed by Epsilon Eridani. However not all the people shared that opinion.

Insurgencies cropped up all over the new Federation, usually no more than a few hundred in an area altogether they caused immense damage and killed thousands of people. Eventually, even Selkd was felled by an assassin at the tender age of 312. His sister Lirdrill was elected to replace him and she was merciless towards the rebels. She named herself "Praetor" and organized the Federal Guard as a military force that would police inhabited space for threats to the Federation, and by extension all Parahumanity. The insurgencies were the first target of this

new force, swiftly and decisively all violent rebels in the stargate network were shot, captured, or annihilated by orbital kinetic bombardment. Captured combatants who had civilian blood on their hands were summarily executed, those who had not were placed in nanostasis and loaded en masse aboard starships with no other form of nanotechnology on board and sent far from the growing empire.
Praetor Lirdrill was praised for her just disposal of the extremists, when elections for her sixth term came around it was whispered that with the still massive distances between stars an election every five years would be impractical, and the legislature passed a law making the position of Praetor last for life. She reigned for another 250 years before retiring, her great-grandson was elected to fill her place. Since then the House of Silver has filled the office of Praetor and many other high offices in the Federation.
It has been seven hundred years since the birth of the Federation, and it still expands to this day. Nearly a hundred systems are connected by the gate network while ten times that number have been contacted or colonized. And the data traders usually manage to keep at least fifty years ahead of the stargates.

The Federation of Parahuman Species:

The Federation, known unofficially as the Centauri Empire or Silver Imperium, is officially a representative democratic confederation but it has some elements resembling more of a constitutional monarchy. While the Core Worlds are fully represented in the congress almost all Praetors of the past seven hundred years have been of the same bloodline and the rim systems not yet connected into the network are frequently treated like the personal fiefdoms of their Federation Emissaries.

Federal Government: The Federal government has three branches as with many 20th century republics. The Executive consists of the Praetor and their advisers, who vary in number with each Praetor. When a Praetor resigns, dies, or is impeached (a very lengthy and convoluted process that has only been completed twice in the Federation's history) a new Praetor is elected by the populace of the stargate network. Campaigning takes five years and every year the candidate pool is winnowed down further and further, the first year the most popular 80 candidates are selected, halved to 40 in the second year, 20 in the third, 10 in the fourth, and finally the Praetor is chosen from the final 5 candidates still in the race. In theory, any citizen of the stargate-connected systems can run, in practice only prominent legislators, planetary politicians, or members of the House of Silver make it past the first year. The Senate has one senator chosen by each planetary government in the network, by whatever means they decide, their primary purpose is to write and debate new laws before passing or rejecting them. The House of Commons, on the other hand, exists to repeal unpopular laws. Representatives of the Commons are elected by each block of 1 million people sectioned out by area every 50 years, 10 candidates are nominated randomly by lottery and 1 is elected by their constituents. 50 years after a law is passed by the Senate it goes before the House of Commons, who vote on whether it should remain or be repealed, if they decide to keep it the law will be reassessed again in another half century.

Ownership: Unlike the majority of 21st century human governments, the Federation is not corporate in nature but is considered the possession of its' head of state, the Praetor. All machinery owned by the Federation from the lowliest guardsman's equipment to the StarForge itself is owned by the Praetor, all state employees work for the Praetor. The Federation usually claims a quarter of a system's natural resources for its' own maintenance and charges taxes from the population for interstellar defense and Gate construction.

The Federal Guard: The Federation's military arm. The Guard is usually the first Federal institution to make its presence known in a system and with good reason. It has two duties: to defend Parahumanity from external threats, and to maintain the unity of the Federation. The first is directed primarily at the Berserkers, piracy is unknown as "trade routes" tend to be light-years long and light-days wide, rendering it nearly impossible to intercept a freighter in transit, and there are few known polities outside the Federation that can threaten it. The Federal Guard has never fought the Berserkers on any known occasion, they tend to enact that duty by stopping long-wave radio transmissions. The second duty is invoked far more often, there is always some group of malcontents somewhere. Standard procedure for dealing with separatists and problematic ideologies is to land power-suited marines directly on bases, armed with less-than-lethal ordinance if the insurgents have not yet killed civilians and lethal weapons if they have, round them all up, execute anyone known to have killed someone, and deport the rest in a ship paid for with the auction of their own assets. It is spelled out quite clearly that secession from the Federation is impossible, emigration, on the other hand, is always an option.

Planetary Governments: While the Federal government is democratic-oligarchic, the governments of individual planets vary a great deal. Democracies, dictatorships, feudal estates, corporate states, it runs the gamut, there may even be multiple governments on one planet. The Federation generally does not care unless 60% of the planet's population petitions for an intervention, in which case the Federal Guard is called upon to overthrow the current government and instate one more to the majority population's liking. This policy has lead to many planets within the stargate network adopting Pallas-style democracies, either gradually or abruptly. Some Out-World Emissaries are suspected of forging or astroturfing intervention petitions.

Ungated Systems: Systems outside the stargate network do not have any sort of representation on SecLand, rather they have an Emissary appointed by the Praetor who acts as a liaison between the planetary governments and the Federation. Predominantly running the local Guard starport. It is not uncommon for Emissaries to set themselves up as military dictators of their planets, but the Congress does send an inspector every so often, depending on how far the system is from the nearest gate and the previous inspector's report. More than one inspector has vanished mysteriously en route to their destination, standard Guard policy is to dispatch an invasion fleet after five disappear.

Economy: The Federation economy is generally capitalistic, discounting planetary governments that attempt more control. There are many currencies in use in its borders, but two are in prominence. The Production credit is backed by an industrial complex that forms the heart of every Federal city, fully robotic, capable of producing most goods with publicly available blueprints, and stocked with a large supply of carbon, oxygen, hydrogen, iron, and silicon. Anyone with credits on account may use them to order goods from this complex. These complexes are also used by the Federal government itself, relieving a bit of the tax burden from the citizenship. Trade credits on the other hand are issued by interstellar merchants when a planet doesn't have a strong currency. Natives sell them goods or data and are paid in trade credit, which they then use to buy data and goods from the traders, or try to exchange them with their neighbors. Other currencies include rare elements, favored by merchants, cryptocurrencies, favored by people who don't expect to leave their native infosphere, and the occasional fiat currency. There are also a few governments with gift or barter economies, though they usually need to actively intervene to prevent the formation of de facto currencies.

As anti-corporate as the Pallene are the Praetor simply cannot be everywhere at once. While the Federation leaves a great deal to local governments to handle anything more than a light-second outside a planet or habitat with a population of 1,000 is their jurisdiction. The Federation also maintains a starport on the most populous body in a system and in the stargate (if present). For example, if Earth were part of the Federation Luna would be under Federal control until it attracted enough colonists to apply for statehood, while Phobos and Deimos would be Martian territory.

That is a great deal of space to administer, as such the Praetor maintains several Federal Bureaus to act in their stead. Each of these Bureaus is led by an Executor appointed by the Praetor, usually on their prior performance within the Bureau though as always there are exceptions. Bureau employees tend to start out at the bottom and work their way up, but cronyism and nepotism are not unknown and a few houses are known for their employment in one Bureau or another.

Ungated systems also have a unique quirk, the Bureaus operating in such systems don't normally answer to their Bureau superiors elsewhere in the Federation, but to the system's Emissary who appoints the local directors much like the Praetor to the Executors.

Major Bureaus:

Bureau of Allocation: Responsible for collecting taxes and budgeting to the other Bureaus. Since collecting taxes from ungated systems is... difficult to say the least, the standard policy for such systems is to spend collected taxes on local projects or on portable assets such as qubits or starships.

Bureau of Defense: The Federal Guard and Civil Guards responsible for defending the Federation from threats both external and internal.

Bureau of Ecology: Evaluates planets for Parahuman inhabitation and approves terraforming projects.

Bureau of Memetic Health: Monitors the emergence and spread of memes that might impact the Federation's cohesion. Calls on the Bureau of Defense when intervention in a meme carrier group is warranted, up to an including exile to the Outworlds.

Bureau of Transportation and Trade: Licenses conversion drive starships, produces the monopoles required for their reactors, and maintains the Starforge and the fleet of linelayers that produce the stargate network.

Bureau of Xenosophont Relations: Formerly the Bureau of Xenoarchaeology. Originally founded to study the remains of extinct alien civilizations, ever since contact with the Kershkans their mandate has been expanded to encompass contact with the Federation's non-Terran client states.

The House of Silver: The family descended from the reconstituted genes of Argentum. The House includes many prominent legislators, administrators, Guard officers, Emissaries, and priests. There are numerous clans and branches of the House scattered throughout the Federation, generally following one of two philosophies. Preservers tend to believe that they should be exerting a tighter grip on the Federation, and have a habit of trying to preserve the founders genes as much as possible. Innovators want to experiment, both with their genotype and with governments. While all Silvers have trace genes from Argentum's companions and lovers the Innovators are known to incorporate scores of other genes, even going so far as to sexually reproduce outside the family on occasion. Features such as wings, taurism, and non-binary sexual characteristics are among the least radical modifications, they are even found among Preservers. Breeding pairs are customarily arranged by House or clan elders for eugenic reasons, and may shift at a moments' notice. This selective breeding has resulted in a bit of mental instability, anyone with a mental disorder more noticeable than a simple antisocial personality disorder is barred from the breeding lists. Some branches surgically sterilize their "rejects" but they can get that fixed in almost any Core World clinic, so instead they disinherit any children they manage to produce. Something they have tried to encourage is the creation of telepaths, each generation has used a combination of drugs and nanotech to induce twinning in at least one pregnancy, frequently resulting in three or more children with identical genes and some degree of mental connection. They use these telepaths to form their own secure FTL communications networks, unfortunately they have an even greater than average (for the House) tendency towards autism spectrum disorders or psychoses, keeping them out of the gene pool.

The Final Battle:

    General Shin, son of Shor, of the House of Frink, Clan Tiger surveyed the battlefield before him. On either side of the field stood a force of parahumans so utterly convinced as to the righteousness of their cause to fight unto their own demises. He fought for the glory of Queen Seria, the duly elected monarch of Schwarswelt, and his cousin. The scum facing him now were the last remnants of the rebel clans who defied the rule of the unified kingdom forged by his great-grandfather Hideo. His forces had hounded them across the continent, facing their warriors in the fields and city streets alike, his spies unveiling clever traps and turning dissatisfied vassals against their lords to join with them. The Rebels had done the same, of course, but with their inferior numbers and weapons it had barely sufficed to hold the Royalists at bay for this long.

    Shin drew out his spyglass and sought out the line moving out of the city towards the trenches hastily constructed to slow down his forces. As he focused he noticed not only soldiers and cavalry warriors, but a significant number of siege tanks. The latter surprised him, the Rebels hadn't acquired the self-propelled armored vehicles until long after his own clan had and conventional battle doctrine placed them at the other end of a siege. Shin replaced his spyglass and checked his own forces' progress on building trenches, they had finished two trenches and were half done with a third, the Rebels would be here within the hour. But what were the Rebels planning with those tanks of theirs?

    The general left his observation post and called for a messenger to find the Pallas envoy and bring her to him. After ten minutes the messenger returned, alone. "The lady's guards say that she is busy meditating and is not to be disturbed."

Shin scowled at the messenger, who wilted under his glare. "Take me to them, I wish to have a word with those guards of hers." After a moment of hesitation the messenger headed off to the far end of the camp, the general following close behind.

Several minutes later the general walked up to a massive tent situated as far from the main battle line as it was possible to be without lying outside the camp's defensive perimeter. Flanking the entrance were two massive parahumans with four legs and two arms and covered head to foot in silver filigree-laced armor that concealed their features. The nearer of the two turned to face Shin as he approached. "The envoy is not to be disturbed at this time." The guard stated flatly.

"This is urgent," General Shin replied. He was unsure of what caste these guards were, or even how the Republic of Pallas' caste system was organized, but most taur clans in Schwarswelt were serfs, and he could not help thinking that he was being told off by a mere peasant. No matter how armored they were. "The battle will be commencing very soon and I need her advice," his voice raised with his aggravation and indignation, "immediately!"

A voice came out from the interior of the tent. "Oh, fine! Let him in." The guards held back the tent flaps for Shin to enter and he did so, with visible annoyance. Envoy Sharlin Fairhold de Argentum was a silver fox, like the rest of Pallas' ruling clan, but her tail had some odd ring-like patterns he'd noticed a few times, and as she hastily donned her robes Shin thought he spotted something on her stomach that he could have sworn was a marsupial pouch. The envoy fastened the edge of her robe and finally addressed him. "Let me guess," she sniped, "you want me to explain once again how to use the technology we gave you because these troublesome insurgents have surprised you?"

General Shin groaned inwardly, the Republic's envoys had always been this dismissive towards the people of the Kingdom, he suspected their government felt the same and kept sending hybrids to them to show it. No matter their claims of "outgrowing" the stigma against interbreeding. He gritted his teeth and told her, "the Rebels are deploying tanks, more than we expected them to have."

"Hmm," Sharlin considered the situation, "it's not too surprising, when you think about it. They've been pillaging archaeological digs for decades, the Lostech artifacts could have easily included armored vehicles or even manufactories. Not to mention the raids on your supply routes to capture your tanks."

The general dismissed the feeling of inadequacy that the envoy tried to project on him. Of course the Ancients would have had weapons to rival those that Pallas had gifted them, the stories indicated the Ancients were no strangers to war while the Republic ludicrously claimed to have fought only a single war in the past millennium. "That wasn't all," Shin continued. "They're defending from a siege, why use them now?"

"Siege?" Sharlin seemed to barely hold herself back from bursting into laughter. "You've had those things for most of a century now and you still think of them as siege weapons?"

"Well, what are they then if not siege weapons?" Shin exclaimed, anger rising. "Please do enlighten this ignorant savage."

"For one thing," Sharlin answered, ignoring the obvious barb, "they can scale the trenches your troops so hastily erected around this little camp as easily as the ones around the city." Shin nodded, he'd considered that possibility but thought the camp's mobility diminished the effectiveness of that plan. "Secondly, they can outpace those lizards your highborn warriors insist on continuing to ride and trample more infantrymen under their treads."

"I had heard something along those lines." Shin admitted, "there was talk about using armored vehicles as warrior mounts but some thought it unfitting for the high-born to rely on common-birth drivers." And also to work siege engines, but he kept that to himself.

'Well, that's a particularly silly move," Sharlin added. "Because the cannons on tanks are better suited to killing tanks than anything your troops or warriors carry on them. You could duel each other to your heart's content."

General Shin froze as he realized what the envoy was telling him, but then his training took over and he dashed back out into the camp. "Messenger!" He called out, and a coyote youth answered. "Rouse the siege tanks men and have them ready their machines to move out. I'll be there to speak with them soon." As the boy ran off, the tiger general considered how rapidly the face of war was changing.

Ten minutes later the first of the tanks were mobilizing out of camp to meet the enemy tanks on the field. The tank crews had met his announcement that they were to engage in the field of battle with mixed reactions. Most of them were species of the craftworks caste; rats, raccoons, foxes, monkeys, etc; rather than warriors like his own species. But while many of the tanks men were worried about the risk of engaging in active battle there were some crews who felt that their efforts had been underappreciated and were eager to finally achieve some glory in combat. It was possible some even held a glimmer of hope that they could be granted warrior status and land rights. That was ludicrous, of course, more likely that once the frontline value of their mounts were realized some of the highborn warriors would be placed in command positions on tanks, if there were enough to fill them.

One of his Lieutenants, a leopardess by the name of Ayami Mercer, sidled up next to Shin, "are you sure about this, General?"

Shin didn't break his view away from the tanks advancing towards each other to address her. "I know it's unconventional," he replied. "But how many other weapons can you name that can penetrate their armor?"

"I don't know their names, but I do know that the Republic's traders offered them." Mercer answered. "Some traders visited my uncle's estate when I was a child and showed off some weapons they wanted to sell. They had a rifle that could punch a hole through half a meter of steel with a single shot, and another gun with three rotating barrels that seemed to spew out bullets like water from a firehose."

The general had heard rumors of similar things, but he wasn't on the board that approved new weapons for the National Army. House Guards, however, were less uniform in armament than the Army, with the wealthier Houses arming their troops with Republic-made guns and armor, while some of the poorest Houses still used crossbows. The fact that the opposition forces were composed of the Guards of all the Houses loyal to the Rebel Clans and that he didn't know what they had armed themselves with was starting to disturb him. He asked her, "did your uncle buy any of those weapons by any chance?"

"He bought one of the rifles for hunting sea-dracols, but he said that the multi-barreled gun was too 'unsporting' or something." The lieutenant replied. "The multi-barrel required two men to carry and needed to be set up on a stand of some kind before firing anyways."

As their tanks approached the forward line of trenches a detachment of infantry rose and advanced ahead of them to clear the way. They had not gone 10 meters when all of a sudden a line of fire erupted from the lead enemy tank, most of it went wide but still a third of the line fell backwards while the rest quickly dropped to the ground and took what cover they could. Shin focused his spyglass on the lead tank and he spied a small secondary turret below the main gun, its barrel seemed to be spinning at high speed as it spat out tracer bullets at an astonishing pace. The Royalist tanks stopped at the loss of their escort, but then one tank raised its main gun high and fired a shell into the air. The others followed suit. Shin pointed out the lead tank's gun seconds before it was smashed by the first of the three shells to strike the vehicle.

"Yes," Mercer confirmed, "that looks like the second weapon the traders showed my uncle." The second shell split open the main turret, and the third detonated the ammo magazine, producing a fireball and shockwave that knocked the surrounding rebel infantry flat. Other shells had similar effects on the rest of the first rank of rebel tanks, stray shells cratered the landscape and scattered infantry, many in pieces. "It seems like a rather undignified way to die, doesn't it?"

"You say that as if there was a dignified way to die." Shin turned to see the Republic's envoy approaching them, flanked by her bodyguards.

General Shin scowled, annoyed beyond reason. "Lady Fairhold," he addressed her, "come to view the fruits of your Republic's labors?"

Sharlin looked slightly confused by his statement. "What could you possibly mean?"

"This!" He exclaimed, pointing at the battlefield. "This destruction, this carnage, all wrought with your weapons."

"Our weapons?" Sharlin Fairhold de Argentum almost seemed to laugh at him. "We haven't sold you any weapons that weren't invented by the humans nearly two thousand years ago. You would have re-invented or salvaged them on your own eventually."

"Don't you try making excuses." General Shin retorted. "You have turned war from a honorable and glorious endeavor into a slaughterhouse. Those tanks aren't even driven by warriors, they're engineers!"

"War? Glorious?" The vulpine ambassador stared incredulously at the tiger general. "You are killing people en masse, does dying from having your guts cut out by a sword rather than a bomb make death any less painful?" She turned to face the continuing battle before them, focusing intently on the tanks.

Shin struggled to come up with a retort as Sharlin stood there and watched the battle. "Men deserve to face their opponent, not just be cut down like wheat or crushed by an unstoppable force."

Sharlin said nothing for several minutes, then said, almost as a non sequitur, "it is fortunate your tanks are driven by engineers rather than warriors. Clearly the enemy lacked that foresight." Shin scanned the cratered surface of the field, none of the Rebel tanks remained intact and their infantry were scattered, the Royalists hadn't even taken to the field. "Because your new chariots are maintained by parahumans with a greater sense of ballistic trajectories than "glory", you have won this battle with minimal loss of life on your side. Try to show some gratitude."

General Shin son of Shor of the House of Frink, Clan Tiger could not bring himself to publicly admit that she was right, even though inwardly he knew it was so.

Core World Planets and Cultures

Alpha Centauri System:
SecLand:
2nd planet from Proxima Centauri
Population: 10 billion
Climate: 10-15% warmer on average than Old Earth, terraformed, multiple biomes.
Orbital Period: .874 Standard Years
Rotation: Accelerated to 24 hours
Government: Mixed Democracy/Oligarchy
History: SecLand, Terra Secundus, New Pallas, The Capital. The first exosolar planet colonized by terragen life and the center of the Federation of Human Species. The first seed ship to SecLand came from the Republic of Pallas in Sol System and immediately set to work building their settlement, known then as "Second Landing" and now as "SecLand Arcology", and a network of observatory satellites and orbital weapons platforms in case future colonists proved hostile, or the great foe that had reduced the Solar System to rubble found them. The second colony ship, this time from the Society for the Preservation of Parahuman Species from Vesta, arrived 25 years later. Hampered, as it were, by the cargo space taken up by their onboard gestation labs and war factories for an anticipated invasion. However, by the time of their arrival the Pallas colonists had built up defenses that gave the crew, already demoralized by the loss of Sol, sufficient pause to consider negotiations. After a quarter of the SPPS crew had been spaced it was agreed that they would set down on the far side of the planet from the Pallas arcology, and their scientists would turn their expertise in biology

to terraforming the then-barren world while New Pallas built up their mutual defenses and infrastructure. The third and final colony ship, this one from Earth and carrying over a thousand live and fully grown humans, arrived fifty years after the first ship. This craft brought a wide range of skills and knowledge, living knowledge, to a planet whose inhabitants up until then had primarily only known life inside their half-built habitat structures. The humans emigrated nearly equally to both colonies, over the centuries they interbred with the parahumans, with the net result being that many SecLanders have less fur or their facial features are closer to human than many further colonies. Today purebred humans, and parahumans (except uplifts), are miniscule minorities on SecLand with only a couple million individuals. The average SecLander resembles a blend of at least half a dozen species of Terragen origin. For centuries the two colonies lived in relative peace, New Pallas breeding like rabbits while the SPPS cloned new citizens in bulk. But when the terraforming of SecLand had reached the point where colonists could breathe the atmosphere tensions re-established themselves between the two old enemies. With terraforming nearing completion some wondered what use New Pallas could have for the SPPS, on both continents. To that end the SPPS began to covertly build weapons in their Arcologies while New Pallas shifted their orbital satellites slightly. The humans of both colonies made a brief attempt to broker a peace, but when the mass-produced faces of the SPPS met the yellow eyes and pointed ears of Pallas they realized that they no longer had much in common as well. It all came to a head when the SPPS concealed a lethal virus in food shipments sent from their farms to the cities of New Pallas, thousands died in the months that followed. By the time the New Pallas government realized what had been done every SPPS arcology had unveiled surface-to-orbit mass drivers that could shoot down their enemy's satellites. Even then, many arcologies were leveled by orbital strikes. Then the land battles began. The cybernetically augmented citizen-soldiers of New Pallas facing off against the bioprinted legions of the SPPS. The fighting raged on for months, then abruptly, it ceased less than a year after the war had begun. The SPPS had underestimated New Pallas's skill with biotechnology, crafting a virus that could be deadly to all the diverse inhabitants of the Republic had been difficult, but a dirty little secret of many 21st century regimes were the techniques to engineer a virus that had disastrous effects when it interacted with a specific gene or genes. And the Society for the Preservation of Parahuman Species had only used a couple genotypes for their army, and even fewer for their ruling priest-scientists. Once the virus had been grown any SPPS unit that came into contact with the enemy was dead within a week, in a month the ruling class had been reduced to a few paranoid individuals who had sealed themselves in hermetic bunkers. Specialized by repeated cloning into an effective caste system, and their soldier castes suddenly extinct, the surviving SPPS arcologies found themselves helpless against New Pallas occupation forces. Their ancestral enemies crushed, the House of Silver turned their sights upward.

Tau Ceti system:
Schwarswelt:
Population: 8.4 billion
Climate: 10% colder on average than Earth, not terraformed, mirror amino native life
Orbital Period: 1.6 Standard years
Rotation: 30 hours
Gravity: 1.2 G
Government: Constitutional Monarchy
History: Shortly after Tau Ceti was settled an ideological movement that believed genotypes must be maintained to prevent homogeny from dooming the species emerged and grew to encompass a significant fraction of the population. The group's solution to the supposed problem was to separate each "species" of parahuman, based on their non-human gene donor, into different "clans" that would settle different regions of the planet. The clans grew in population rapidly, bumping up against the borders designated at founding in less than a century. War broke out. Clans rallied behind charismatic warrior-nobles and weaker clans swore oaths of fealty to stronger ones to save their own skins. These wars continued until contact with the first probe from the Centauri system, realizing that there was another civilization out there and that they were capable of interstellar travel the clan heads held a council to decide what to do about it. The majority ruled that they needed a single man to represent their world when the outsiders came in person, they elected King Hideo Fink of the feline clan as the official ruler of Tau Ceti. When the official diplomatic envoys and information merchants arrived he dealt with them, when the first stargate was constructed his granddaughter negotiated the terms for the merger of the two world governments. But many in the major clans resented the loss of their sovereignty to first another clan who hadn't even had the courtesy of beating them in battle and now to these off-worlders? They re-organized their armies and led assaults on the Federation enclaves. Praetor Lirdrill did not tolerate this defiance and sent the first units of the newly mustered Federal Guard to suppress these rebels. Surprisingly, she and the king of Tau Ceti found unexpected allies in many of the minor clans

subordinate to the rebels. These minor clans had been exposed to the democratic ideals of SecLand and saw an opportunity to gain some measure of independence in the brewing war. This set the precedent for future "interventions" in planetary government by the Federation. When the dust was settled the surviving rebel elements of the clans were deported beyond the present borders of the Federation and a parliament was set up to govern Tau Ceti. Each clan, major or minor, is represented equally in the upper house of parliament while the lower house represent geographical regions by population independent of clan. It has been that way ever since, despite grumbling by old conservatives and young romantics, both are free to leave for colonies where feudalism is still practiced.

Epsilon Eridani
Population: 4.2 billion
Climate: 30% warmer than old Earth, partial terraforming. High CO_2 content
Orbital Period: .6 standard years
Rotation: 108 hours
Government: Technocratic corporate state
The third of the "Core" worlds, Eridani has been shaped by its long history just as much as its "sister" systems. Settled by one of the last colony ships out of Sol, the crew was left in a panic by the sudden destruction of the world they had left behind and thought they should keep running. However, their ship had only been designed for a one-way trip and could not hold out far beyond their intended destination of Epsilon Eridani, they not only would need to stop for refueling and repairs, they'd need to rebuild the ship entirely. They set up a colony on the most habitable (if barely) planet in the star system and dedicated as much of the infrastructure as possible to building a new starship. As the biofabbed workforce grew the crew realized that they could use the planet as a starting point for many more colony ships that could spread parahumanity across the cosmos. When the first new ship was complete half the original crew left aboard it, the other half stayed behind to direct construction of later ships and train the biofabbed (and their natural-born descendants) to crew them. Over the centuries more and more habitats were constructed to exploit new mineral deposits all over the star system and the population grew. Their single-minded purpose and the hostility of the natural environment made a totalitarian government seem a necessity, but the founders impressed upon them a necessity for the finest minds to be recognized. The government was essentially a single monopolistic company devoted to making starships, the highest ranked

engineers decided the fate of the colony, promotion was, in theory, meritocratic. In practice Eridani became a familial oligarchy like so many others who came before them, half of whose highest echelons left the planet behind every generation. Dozens of colony ships were launched before contact with Centauri, Eridani colonies are still found every so often. It was a simple arrangement for the two worlds, Centauri had advanced propulsion and communication technologies, Eridani had a star system devoted to building ships, both wanted to spread their people out across the galaxy, they gave little trouble when the system was admitted to the Federation. Now, Eridani is the Federation's primary center for building starships, most of the Federal Guard's warships and countless mercantile craft were built there. The system has almost as many stargates as Centauri, freighters carrying rare elements for shipbuilding coming in from the frontier regions, and new freighters going out to their new owners throughout the Federation. However, a number of Centauri have emigrated to Eridani looking for work, whose democratic ideals threaten to shake the foundation of their technocratic society.

Family Ties

I wasn't sure what was more surprising, that the Praetor himself would call upon a lowly private investigator like myself, or that he would call me the day after I saw his assassination on the evening newsfeeds. It had been the top story for the past 20 hours, I must have seen clips of that fox's blood boiling from his ears and staining his black and white fur a dozen times since then. They said that his microbots had been hacked by his own doctor, instead of maintaining his brain and body against the ravages of age, they disintegrated his neural tissue. Even the best medical science of the Federation could not repair that much brain damage. Fortunately for my state of mind, he explained how he managed this feat of self-necromancy a second after I answered.
"I am the personality simulation of Praetor Senyan Terraformer de Argentum a Denal, carrying out my last will and testament." That figured, of course someone as rich and powerful as a Praetor would be capable of commissioning a personal sim, and now that I thought about it, most of the ones I'd seen before were former Praetors or other notable members of the Argentum genus. "In the event of my death by the intent of another being, I set aside a sum of 100 kiloPCs to hire the most qualified private investigator available to determine the identity of whomever was ultimately responsible for my death."
"Well, that's interesting," I replied, "but what makes you think I'm the most qualified for the job?"
The simulation perked as I'd clearly triggered some sort of response path. "You are the private investigator known as 'Rikel Eryn' are you not? Primary phenotype: Feline. Birthplace: Ceti outcast colony #283, date:

approximately 4/18/1727 Most notable profession: Detective experienced roughly 126 years?"

Pretty much accurate, I admit. It was rather difficult to synchronize the calendars of the various outlier worlds with those of the core worlds linked by the wormhole nexus, but that was close enough for my purposes. I had started my career as a professional finder of evidence for criminal cases before I had become an immortal Federation citizen, back on that primitive little mudball the Federation had dubbed "Ceti colony #283" but most of its inhabitants called "dirt", having been there long enough to forget that there were other inhabited planets in the universe. Still, there was the occasional contact with offworld traders that the government tried to keep secret. I'd come across a group of these offworlders on one of my cases, and had no choice but to leave with them or be "disappeared" by the Emperor's agents.

It was rather uncommon for anyone, mortal or immortal, to hold down the same career for more than fifty years by the capital's reckoning. Those born to the Federation grew up accepting the idea that they'd get bored doing the same thing for decades on end and couldn't imagine keeping it up for centuries, but on my former home planet people were expected to stick with the same career for life. To be honest, we'd only just recently moved past the species-based caste system espoused by the original colonists.

I confirmed the digital ghost's assessment, not bothering to explain why I'd been in this job so long, and asked why it wanted my help. "After all," I explained, "you have the full resources of the civil forces and the Federal Guard to investigate the cause of your demise."

"The civil forces and the Federal Guard are presently under the control of my kin." The simulation answered. "And I believe one of them was responsible."

For a brief time I thought I'd left such things behind when I ditched my old planet. Here where there's so little need for struggle and strife, and cameras are everywhere so you can't get away with anything, I thought this world would be free of murder. But of course, that wasn't quite the case. I mean, sure, there's a much lower violent crime rate, but there's still some things that people find to be worth killing over. And, just like back home, it was often the ones with the most to gain who were most likely to think they could get away with murder.

Unfortunately for me, the Praetorian succession wasn't a straight line like most major titles on my home. Technically, it was elected, but everyone knew that only the high families of the genus Argentum had the Federation-wide influence to win. Even if I narrowed down the possible suspects to Senyan's immediate family I ended up with more than 50 offspring by a dozen different mates and 19 siblings to investigate. Even with AI search agents it was a long list to work through.

While my software ran through the list of potential masterminds, I decided to approach the case from the other end. The civil authorities had determined that the parahuman who metaphorically "pulled the trigger" was the Praetor's personal physician, Keltin de Natalie a Jonah. Unfortunately for my investigation he had already been tried and executed, rather rapidly I might suppose. Prevailing theory was that he was involved in some new cult or something, that being the default media bogeyman ever since the Memetic Quarantine Act that got my ancestors and so many other "deviants" dumped on some frontier world with no real technology. Conveniently, the Act also placed a media block on any details of the perpetrators of suspected ideological terrorism, on the grounds that the information might carry a meme virus, as it was I was lucky to find his name so quickly.

The major news sites had been given enough information to know that Senyan's doctor was believed to have done the deed, but nothing about the doctor's identity. I'd found a news article that was over fifty years old about the Praetor's new physician. Keltin was of musteline ancestry, some weasel blend, Centauri-born and bred, and his name was on the public citizen's record as having died about a week after the Praetor. I also couldn't find any record of Senyan changing doctors in the last half-century so it was most likely him. What confirmed it was the lack of information on any official site that would have told me something about him. Nothing on the Wikipedia Stellaria, nothing on the university that the news page said he studied at, nothing from the "notable personages" of the Natalie or Jonah genera. At least, until I did some digging into the past. You see, the thing about a decentralized network like the Federation mesh, it's really hard to destroy any information in its totality. A few queries on secure networks and I had archived copies of every page that had information on Keltin de Natalie a Jonah, I even found some cracker who had his transaction records up to the month before he killed.

Technically, it was an anonymous wallet, but it was accessed through his BCI which pretty much meant it was his. And there's a little thing about cryptocurrencies like the Federation's Production Credit that many people seem strangely ignorant of, they remember who has owned them. Every FedPC file that changes virtual hands has something called a "blockchain" which carries the ID number of every wallet it has passed through. There's no database with the ID of every cryptocurrency wallet in use in the Federation core worlds or anything like that, but a lot of people put their wallet ID on their personal sites in public view so people can send them money. The largest transaction on the record was a deposit two weeks ago from a source that I couldn't quite identify, but followed a day later by an almost as large withdrawal to a wallet that I quickly tied to a discount cybersurgeon in one of the outlying small towns by the name of Lucas Kelner.

Kelner had moderate online reviews on the mesh, but comparing his lifestyle to what he would have made off the jobs the reviews mentioned something did not add up. I figured he had to be taking some work on the "greyer" side of things to afford that interstellar vacation he took photos of on social media. I decided to pay "Dr. Kelner" a visit and took a maglev train out to the town.

His office was near the edge of the city limits, I noticed a distinct lack of sousveillance sensors in the area, the only ones around seemed to be tied to Kelner's building and thus under his control. It was a cheap pre-fab, the kind that lasted barely more than a few decades and would need to be replaced fairly soon, but was enough to exert ownership over a plot of land. I went in through the front door and spoke to the owner.

His digital receptionist kept me waiting for almost a half hour before letting me see him. Lucas Kelner was a cervine male who had replaced his antlers with a pair of fractal arms, branching off into increasingly small armatures tipped with a variety of tools and jacks for surgical instruments. "Good afternoon, sir", he said as I was let into his office room and took a seat. "How may we improve you today?"

"Actually," I replied, "I was wondering if you could tell me anything about one of your recent clients."

I noticed a small nervous twitch as my question registered with him. "There are customer reviews of my work on several sites."

"I'm wondering about one who didn't post any reviews." I continued, calmly. "One Keltin de Natalie a Jonah."

Kelner looked very nervous at this point. "Some of my clients appreciate their privacy. They pay additional credits to keep the details between the two of us and I am not inclined to betray their trust." Something wasn't quite right, his ear was flicking back and forth and I couldn't tell why.

"Listen," I warned him, "this is very important and if you don't share the information I'm looking for there could be very dire consequences. And not just for you." He shuddered as I spoke to him.

Then suddenly, he coughed loudly, making me jump for a second. As he drew his hand back from his mouth I thought I saw something red glisten across his palm. "It looks like there'll be consequences if I tell too."

Without warning he jumped at me, barely missing as I leapt out of the way just in time to avoid the bared scalpels on his bionic antlers. Despite appearances, Kelner wasn't the only augmented parahuman in the room. Since emigrating to the Federation I had not only installed the standard BCI and longevity microbots, but I'd also had my peripheral nerves myelinated to an almost extreme degree and attached an autonomic override module to my spine. If my BCI picked up a threat it would send the appropriate signals to my override and my body would react before my conscious mind, or even my biological reflexes with their boosted neurons, could register it. There's been a few embarrassing situations in the past but the mods have saved my not-quite-immortal life often enough to make up for them.

I stood there in the office ducking and weaving automatically to avoid having any of the cyborg cervine's surgical instruments hit me, or get any of his bodily fluids on me. A much more difficult task now that blood was streaming out of his nose and ears. At one point one of his graspers grabbed something off the back of his head and threw it at me, the override made me catch it and throw it aside before it could do anything. I jumped past Kelner to land on top of his desk as he started to collapse, the microbots in his system finally disintegrating his neurons to the point where he could no longer stand.

The manner of death was too similar to the Praetor's to be a coincidence. If it were the same his hacked microbots would break down his brain into an unrecognizable mush within the hour and the rest of his tissues would follow over the course of the next day. Senyan's body had only been presentable enough for a funeral due to the quick application of an electromagnetic pulse strong enough to fry all the electronics in his body, one bodyguard who'd tried to save him without putting on gloves first had to have an arm amputated and all her cyberware replaced. Seeing how de Natalie was dead I was certain now that something wasn't quite what it seemed.

I tried to remember exactly when Kelner had started showing signs of hostile microbot infection. Then, not trusting my suggestible meat brain I called up the last few minutes of my Lifelog. Like many people over a hundred years old I knew full well the limitations of flesh memory and had taken the easy route of setting my BCI up to record all input from my senses to an external memory drive at the base of my skull. Most nights before going to bed I reviewed my Lifelog and backed up important events to a personal cloud server that I could access from the mesh as needed. But sometimes I witnessed something sensitive which I would not want to be accessible from the mesh at all so I physically removed the memory cylinder and stashed it in a Faraday safe.

As I was reviewing my memories of the fight I got to the point where

Kelner threw that thing at me. I paused the memory to get a better look at the object, and to my surprise I found that it was a memory cylinder, of a similar type to the ones I used in fact. Quickly I followed the arc my hardware remembered to where the cylinder had landed under a bookshelf and recovered it. The ports were a bit dusty but it was intact and free of microbot-contaminated fluids, I counted myself lucky that he wasn't one of those types who thought sanitary access panels were unsightly, if he'd used a wireless BCI like many people these days I doubt I'd have been able to safely dig his external memory out of his skull before the microbots destroyed it.

The cylinders I used could hold a month's worth of memory, if Kelner hadn't changed or overwritten this one in the two weeks since he'd operated on de Natalie I could have just found my first bit of hard evidence.

I left Kelner's disintegrating body in his office, with any luck the civil authorities wouldn't notice until after I'd solved this case. Now I had a lead to follow. Normally, external memory can only be used by the person who made it, biological brains are too different for the same code to be interpreted by anyone else, but there are some programmers who can make a rough translation and review a fuzzy version of someone's else's memories. Naturally, I know one who was willing to help, and who preferred to remain anonymous to protect her identity as this was slightly on the illegal side of things.

I gave her the cylinder and she slipped into a work simulation to translate the memories. While I waited for her to finish I started making inquiries to sousveillance streams on the streets and aisles surrounding the Families' arcology looking for signs of Dr. de Natalie. There were enough free streams to get a general idea of where he had gone in the past month, and the fees to get the details were inconsequential compared to the potential pay for this job. I found that he had gone to a variety of different nightclubs and bars roughly every once or twice a week in the weeks before his death, never the same place twice and with no discernable connection between the establishments. I started looking into the other patrons of those establishments, no one other person had attended all of the same places as him but my recognition software did notice a few mustelids who appeared more than twice, all of whom had the same gait, and one of which was a brightly striped pine marten with three tails.

While it wasn't uncommon to have extra tails added they were associated with one particular subculture of note, Kitsune, those who used nanotech to alter their appearance at will and used the number of tails in their "base form" as a measure of how far they'd progressed in the mental discipline used to control their technological powers. Fortunately my contacts had indicated that they didn't learn how to alter the way they walked until the fifth tail, it was likely that all of the recurring weasels were the same shapeshifter.

Unfortunately, while they had used the same body more than once they had also used a different name each time, and the Kitsune order kept the true identities of their members a secret for their protection. I would have to hope that my interpreter found a hint of their true name in the memories she reviewed.

She was working on those memories for a full day before she got back to me. When she reported her findings her expression was grave, quite clearly rather shaken by what she had seen. "Lucas Kelner implanted a remotely triggered explosive into the cerebral cortex of Dr. Keltin de Natalie a Jonah. Crude, but it would effectively annihilate his brain and external memory beyond any hope of recovery. And it used a quantum-entangled remote so it wouldn't be traceable in any way. When he was done de Natalie injected Kelner with a syringe of the hacked microbots that killed him later."

It didn't make much sense for somebody to willingly implant a remote self-destruct in their own body, there were easier ways to commit suicide. I figured whoever had given de Natalie the money for the procedure had arranged it to prevent him backing out or snitching later, and that he'd placed similar leverage against Kelner. There was definitely more to this than it first seemed. "Did either of them mention who had paid for this invasive surgery, by any chance?"

"Yes," she replied, visibly trying to maintain her calm. "De Natalie said that 'Ryllidin Everstead' would appreciate it if he kept this to himself." She actually looked scared now. "I looked them up on the Darkmesh, they're a Kitsune who's been linked to some unpleasant things. What kind of person hires you for this kind of job?"

"The ghost of Senyan Terraformer de Argentum a Denal." I said, half sarcastically.

"Don't be ridiculous." She snapped. "He couldn't have had a simulation made, he was a Telepath."

I paused, curious. "You mind explaining what you mean by that?"

"To make a simulation of a person, you need to do two things." She informed me. "First, you need to have a BCI recording a Lifelog, and second, you need to get a high-def brain scan to make a computer model capable of interpreting that Lifelog." Even I did not need to be told that having a machine read a Telepath's brain would break their connection to their bonded twin, reducing them from a vital component of interstellar

communications to a mundane member of Federation society.
I had not known this about Senyan, but now I had a hunch on who killed him, and I was willing to stake my life on it.

The bar was crowded and noisy, dozens of parahumans and uplifts getting intoxicated on a hundred different substances and chatting each other up. I had staked out a booth in the corner and placed a white noise generator under the table, obscuring whatever I would say to the casual observer. Halfway into my first drink Ryllidin Everstead arrived. They were in one of the more nondescript forms I had seen on the streams, an androgynous common brown weasel in a black dress suit. They sat down and we chatted about meaningless things while our hearing adjusted to the noise generator, then once I could understand what they were babbling about the Z-G fights we got down to business.

"So," I interjected, "I hear you're the one to go to when you need a 'job' done right?"

"I find the right people." Ryllidin corrected me. "I act as an intermediary between clients who wish to remain anonymous and the people they don't want associated with them. You give me the details, and I find the workers who can get it done. They don't know who you are just as much as you don't know who they are."

"Plausible deniability," I said, "nice." Now, I offered a hypothetical. "So, you mean to say that if, for instance, a member of one of the Families wanted his twin brother dead you would be the only one who knew who was ultimately behind it and everyone who was involved in the assassination attempt?"

Everstead didn't even flinch. "Hypothetically, yes. That would be the case. But you don't need something that drastic now do you?" My senses picked up some slight movement under the table, but my override didn't think it a threat yet.

I pushed further. "What if someone found the workers and tortured or paid them to find your location? I mean, nowadays even with the shapeshifting they can find out who you are with little effort."

"Oh, I have methods of making sure they can't talk." Whatever they were moving became fast enough that my override registered a threat and reacted. I lunged across the table just as an abnormally long finger whipped out a dataport connector of some kind. They were pinned to the seat beneath me as the connector clattered on the table. I struggled to pin them down as they writhed beneath me, joints dislocating to wriggle out, I lost my grip for just a moment but that was enough for Everstead to get free. Their suddenly prehensile tail snatched the thing off the table but a random corsac fox in the crowd abruptly grew three-inch claws on his

left hand and sank them into the fleeing weasel's torso.
I winced as the crook I'd been trying to catch suffered serious internal organ damage but didn't make a sound. The clawed fox motioned for me to follow him as he led the Kitsune weasel out the back door, all while the crowd acted like nothing was happening.
As soon as we were out of sight of the bar's patrons the fox's fur changed in color from a mixture of yellow and grey to black underfur with white guard hairs, the characteristic coat of the founder that zir Federation-ruling descendants all shared. Then as I watched amazed as his, no her body mass shifted away from the shoulders and abdomen to round out her breasts and hips, and her one tail split in eight. Everyone knew the highest rank of the Kitsune order was nine tails, and that there was only one confirmed nine tail in known space though rumor had it there were more outside the stargate network. This being was in line to head the entire shapeshifting organization, and she was a Silver, in retrospect I should have been much more afraid.
"What do you want?" I asked, wary.
The Silver vixen dangled the limp weasel to the side while she turned to face me. "You can call me Sharlin Fairhold de Argentum. Does that sound familiar?"
I had to think for a minute before I recalled that name. "You were one of Praetor Senyan's mates, weren't you?"
"Yes." She replied simply. "While we didn't quite get along that well he was still the sire of a dozen of my progeny and I'm obligated to get to the bottom of his murder. Now," she said gesturing a lengthening claw at me, "I believe you were saying something about my ex-mate's twin wanting him dead?"
I thought carefully before explaining my running hypothesis. "Praetor Senyan's simulation hired me to solve the case of his murder, but he was a telepath which would normally preclude creating a simulation. After realizing that I did some digging and found a short-lived rumor that he had installed a BCI around thirty years ago, just a couple years after he was elected." Considering what to say next took some time but when I found my voice again I added something that I had only speculated so far. "I don't know what it's like to share your mind with the most powerful being in the galaxy but I can't imagine he took it well when his brother suddenly became the most known entity to everyone in the Federation while he remained out of the public eye."
"Resulting in a falling-out so drastic that he would intentionally sever a bond he's had since before he was born?" Sharlin suggested. Her grip on Everstead tightened and the blood flowing from her wounds intensified. "I was a telepath too, you know. The eugenics board wanted to produce

more FTL communications nodes by having them breed with one another. When I was chosen to mate with Senyan I could feel my sister's envy, but we worked it out and went back to being closer than any two individuals have any business being after I got pregnant with octuplets." She let her face show some glimmer of emotion before resuming her prior stoicism. "Then she died in a skimmer accident, I felt a flash of pain and then, nothing. She was just gone, it felt like I'd lost everything, but every part of my body was still there. In an attempt to cope I joined the Kitsune order and submerged myself in the training, I didn't get to eight tails in just 300 years solely from connections you know."

I guessed that the Kitsune's specialized implants were also incompatible with telepathy, they would at the very least need a BCI to control the rest. "Isn't that thing," I gestured towards the barely conscious body in her hand, "another one of your order?"

She briefly looked back, "we exist to sow chaos, to keep civilization from growing stagnant and decaying from idleness. Now, I have no problem with causing a hiccup in monopole production or introducing an anthropophagic symbiont to a regressed planet, but assassinating the Praetor and replacing him with a fratricidal maniac is too much. Someone that unstable in charge could spell the end for the parahuman species." Sharlin sighed, "now, I know that you're a bit suspicious of the House of Silver, but the general population's reverence for our dynasty is one of the pillars of the Federation. If we lose it the only interstellar civilization in the known universe faces collapse."

I wasn't too sure about that, my own "regressed planet" had survived its' share of mad rulers. But we were somewhat short of world-ending technology like the average Federation starship. "So, what do you plan to do with them?" I asked.

Sharlin thrust the extended claw she'd pointed at me with into Ryllidin Everstead's brainpan through the jaw. They died instantly. "I'll dispose of this one, and we'll take care of Yaznar when he gets here for the election." By which she meant Yaznar Terraformer de Argentum a Denal, Senyan's underappreciated twin who had been assigned to the communications department of some ungated system that had been in the Federation for just a century or so. "As for Dr. de Natalie," out of nowhere she produced the dataport jack that Everstead had taken out, "I presume this is the qubit toggle for the bomb in his head, which as you should know is currently cryonically preserved after separation from his body in accordance with standard capital punishment procedures. In a hundred and fifty years his case will be up for review and he might get a chance at a new body if judged to have been falsely accused, or under duress." She palmed the toggle again. "It would probably be best if this

wasn't publicly known until then. How much did my ex's ghost offer you?"
I shrugged. "100 K."
"I'll match it if you keep this all to yourself for at least 149 years."
Seeing how she'd just casually killed someone permanently I thought it best to take her offer without further complaint.

So yeah, that was back in 1711 Post Exodus, it's now 1860. I kept my word, earned two hundred thousand Production Credits (before deducting the not inconsiderable costs of the whole thing), and stayed alive. Yaznar arrived at Alpha Centauri a month and a half later, coming off of a 25-year voyage with what some noted as convenient timing, and died a day later. The official story was that he committed suicide with an explosive bullet, but I have my own suspicions.

Less than a century later there was a popular rebellion on my homeworld. Though the rebels made no secret of the off-world technology they used they stopped just short of a full coup, the surviving Daimyos agreed to sign a charter instating laws more palatable to the Federation. It took only a generation for the world, now called "Hikar", to be admitted. I believe a stargate is well on its way to the system. Before long the descendants of those I left behind all those centuries ago will get the same core worlds experience I've had for the majority of my life now, for better or for worse.

Otherwise, little has changed. Explored space expands about one lightyear for every three years that pass on the capital. New planets are colonized, whether voluntary or involuntary. And the House of Silver holds the Federation together in the face of internal strife and the monstrosities that destroyed the original planet "Dirt", or "Earth" as they called it in the old tongue.

I suppose, that's the best we can hope for.

Language:

The diaspora and isolation has resulted in the evolution of countless new languages, English alone has spawned hundreds. Fortunately translation software is quite freely available and most Federation citizens have at the very least Augmented Reality glasses, if not cranial implants. Ships on which every crewman speaks a different language and does not know any of their shipmates' tongues are not unknown, but very uncommon. The Federation has made numerous attempts to encourage solidarity and interplanetary cooperation by formulating a single "common tongue", three of which are in common use. Lojban is the official language of business and politics, however its incredible preciseness and linguistic isolation has prevented it from becoming an "everyday" language and its mostly used for contracts and laws. Basic Anglic is a simplified version of English with all regional jargon stripped out and grammar greatly simplified. Anglic spelling is completely phonetic (funetik) with no silent letters or compound sounds. It is fairly commonly used for communication between individuals from different worlds and is probably the most prevalent "second language" and even a first language in some places, as a result it has mutated considerably. Landlish is the naturally evolved language of SecLand, developed from a mix of English, Latin, Mandarin, and Lojban. It's fiendishly complicated to learn as an adult but most inhabitants of the capital only know Landlish and maybe a smattering of Lojban and Anglic, and they've spread it to most planets linked by stargates.

Mercenaries:

Generally speaking, interstellar travel outside the stargate network is uncommon, many systems go years without seeing a starship. Still, a small minority of people make their living voyaging from star to star. These nomads generally fall under one of three categories: traders, explorers/researchers, and military. The third category probably has the largest population at a given time but also the highest turnover rate.

The Federal Guard is the only governmental military with interstellar reach, though they tend to act more like a police force than military, lacking enemies with even close to comparable power. The few outworlds with space navies are usually no match for even a civilian Federation freighter, and the Destroyers are so dreaded that the Guard's standing orders in case of an encounter are to evacuate as many civilians as possible before retreating at full throttle. It's common for restless citizens to sign up for a 50-year term of duty (up to 80% of the time spent in stasis) with the Guard, then transition back to civilian life almost seamlessly. Those who find that they enjoy the interstellar life may sign up for another term or seek employment as a trader or explorer. Others may have been expecting more "action" when they signed up, or actually were in combat once or twice and found they enjoyed it a bit too much. Those parahumans might end up going private.

Private Military Contractors have only three legal roles in Federation space: claim protection, colony security, and training, and a company with a long-term contract may end up filling all three in sequence.

Before a colony is established there is a lot of preparatory work to do, and with the spotty nature of interstellar communications more than once has a planetary claim been grabbed by another group before the one who first filed the claim even had the chance to launch. While there's usually enough room on a planet for multiple colonies these "misunderstandings" tend to result in a lot of friction, and so settlement companies might hire mercenaries to land first and enforce their claim. These mercenaries will typically receive the job notice on the stargate's laser network and the company stationed closest to the destination system will generally get the job, most colonists come from the more densely populated core worlds while PMCs tend to find the most employment out on the frontier, it's convenient. Upon arriving the mercenary company will deploy orbital sensor and weapons platforms and nanofab an air-droppable forward base from an asteroid or two. Most of the company will remain in stasis until another ship arrives though a few will remain awake in shifts to watch for intruders or suppress hostile fauna if the planet is habitable without terraforming. If a ship that doesn't belong to their clients arrives after them the interlopers can usually be turned back, disappointed but unharmed. Still, there's little to no oversight out there on the edges of the frontier and more than once the would-be claim jumpers have have tried taking the planet by force. There are also rumors of mercenary companies that arrived to find claim jumpers already entrenched in the system, with messy but unconfirmed results.

After the colony has been established the PMCs can act as the colony's home guard, defending the settlement from bandits or pirates, occasionally helping settle disputes within the colony or with rivals. When the colony gets around to founding their own home guard the mercenaries help to train them. Once that final phase is complete the mercenary company will typically collect their pay, with all the interest accumulated, and leave. Most of the time they'll work with agents in the core worlds who will forward them job contracts via a quantum link and will have a new contract waiting before they finish their last one.

Outside the Federation's borders, however, all bets are off. The Federal Guard maintains a small patrol in any outworld system, often just a single cruiser/AKV carrier, but so long as no one brings non-implanted nanotech down to the planet's surface they usually won't take notice. For long-term campaigns mercenary companies will plant a nanofab seed in the system's asteroid belt and use it to manufacture their supplies and armory, air-dropping when needed, similar to how most traders sell physical products to primitive worlds.

In the outworlds there are far fewer restrictions on what mercenaries can and can't do, missions range from securing sites for trade enclaves to outright conquest. Some outworld governments may have limited access to the Federation's communications network and use it to hire mercs for wars with other powers on the same planet. Unscrupulous traders may find a given outworld nation's policies "troublesome" and want them "persuaded". Or a Crusader sect of the Noospherists could see an opportunity to "civilize" some "ignorant savages", in fact Crusaders frequently form mercenary companies for this very purpose.

When fighting outworlders mercenaries usually find themselves highly outnumbered but much better armed as even the least regressed outworlds lack access to nanofabbed materiel or medical microbots. However, there's always the risk of a lucky bullet scrambling the brainpan beyond the ability of microbots to repair or worse, the enemy also hiring mercenaries. For those reasons many mercs call it quits after their first mission in the outworlds, taking only Federation-space contracts or quitting the soldier-of-fortune life altogether and returning to civilian life, assuming that they have access to a ship going back into Federation-space that is.

Naming Conventions

The worlds of the Federation and beyond exhibit a panoply of cultures influenced by all manner of civilizations from Earth and some that have been attempts at inventing a culture from scratch. The distinctions between cultures may not be more apparent anywhere than their names. Tau Ceti traditionalists tend towards a patronymic and their species name, Epsilon Eridani assigns every citizen a number that used to be their equivalent to names pre-contact. While the people of New Pallas in Alpha Centauri have come up with a naming system that perplexes many newcomers.

Most Pallene have 3-4 names, all but one of which are hereditary. As an example, Jarlin Fairhold de Argentum a Denal. In zir case Jarlin is zir given name, or praenomen in the Roman terminology. Fairhold is the cognomen, a sort of surname indicating direct descent from a notable ancestor, cognomen may be patrilineal or matrilineal with some taking two or more cognomen.

The last two names are the genera, names tied to the two bits of DNA that pass from generation to generation virtually unchanged. First is the m-genus, fixed to zir mitochondrial plasmids and inherited matrilineally, generally prefixed with "de" or "of". The second is the y-genus tied to

Tales of the Para-Imperium

the y-chromosome prefixed with "a" or "from".

This complicated naming system has its' origins in the Traveller, the Old Pallas seedship that first settled Alpha Centauri. With their knowledge of genetics they knew that any specific genes would be mingled and scattered among any individual's descendants, with the exception of mitochondrial or Y-chromosome genes. The ship's crew being an equal mix of male and female they could not agree on which would be used and adopted the two-genus system as a compromise. As such, names were tied to each of the 500 mitochondria and 250 Y-chromosomes carried within the seedship's genebanks. However, as time passed and the population grew, many desired a means of differentiating each other further. To this end came the practice of adding cognomen to the parenomen and genera.

In the modern interstellar age, every one of the original genera have millions of members, some immigrants have even attempted to establish their own, but three m-genera and two y-genera are of particular note. Derived from the Traveller's crew themselves.

The most famous, of course, is genus Argentum, the descendants of the founder of the Pallas Republic, most of them are at least part vulpine but the families that are most politically active: Tellis, Fairhold, Kolnen, etc, tend towards phenotypes that are at least 75% silver fox. Genus Olga is the second most prestigious m-genus, descended from Pallas' military commander, mostly lupine but much more diverse and less politically active. Genus Natalie, the "forgotten" crew genus, are descended from the one member of the seedship's crew who wasn't the child of the Pallas founding personages, an otter by the name of Natalie; today the genus includes all sorts of mustelidae mixed with practically every species included in the parahuman genome, and those who still care about such things are a bit bitter.

Both of the highest y-genera carry the chromosomes of founding personages, male-line descendants of the Traveller's y-carrying crew. Genus Denal is the larger and more popular of the two, descending from Olga's mate, though repeated intermarriage between genera Argentum and Olga has made the y-genus the most common among praetors of the Federation. Genus Maximus have an unbroken line from Argentum's mate, but the fact that he was a clone of the founder of the SPPS has made the name somewhat less popular.

Core Technology

Conversion Drive: The primary means of interstellar travel in the Federation and most surrounding systems. Magnetic monopoles are passed through a mass of hydrogen, the atoms the monopoles come into contact with are converted to antimatter which reacts with the surrounding hydrogen, catalyzing a fusion reaction that provides thrust. In theory it is safer than normal antimatter-catalyzed fusion in that it does not require carrying a large quantity of antimatter but merely a small amount of re-usable monopoles. The thrust achievable is far greater than normal fusion torches and acceleration exceeds that of solar sails. A typical cruising speed for interstellar voyages is half the speed of light, but velocities up to .7c have been recorded.

Casimir Thruster: In the early 21st century a low-thrust reactionless drive was discovered, it took most of that century to make practical use of the concept though. Regardless, it became invaluable to space travelers. Ships did not need to carry as much bulky reaction mass, all they needed now was a power plant and fusion power had made that far more simple. It was nowhere near fast enough for interstellar travel within the projected lifespan of civilization, and it could not provide enough thrust to rise more than a few centimeters above the ground of an Earth-size planet, but it was enough for regular travel within a star system.

Stargates: A typical stargate is a ring with a 10-kilometer diameter. But the actual mouth of the wormhole is a 500-meter sphere located at the precise center of the stargate. The stargate has no control over the actions of the wormhole, it simply marks its location and provides a base for the Federal Guard who defend the wormhole, or the system on the far side. Ships can enter a wormhole from any angle and come out the other mouth, but for convenience's sake most stargates are oriented perpendicular to the solar system's plane so that ships coming from a planet in the system can make a more-or-less straight run through the ring. They rocket out from one star system, pass through a wormhole, and keep on going into the interior of the next system. Most details on the construction of wormholes are considered top secret, but what has been revealed is that when the route is first laid down the wormhole is very narrow, measured in nanometers, and the mouths are transported in magnetic bottles. When both mouths are in place they are released and large quantities of "exotic matter" are fed into the more coreward mouth, somehow, this props the wormhole open and expands it slowly over the course of several years before finally it reaches its full .5km diameter. For some unknown reason every wormhole mouth has been placed no less than 100 astronomical units from a celestial body of planetoid size or greater, there are many hypotheses why this is, most of them are not good. Some say that wormholes are inherently unstable and only need a little "push" to explode with enough force to shatter nearby planets, others say that they conflict with significantly sized gravity wells, or perhaps the Federation wants to delay potential invaders who might think of using their technology against them, a lot of people think it's a mixture of all three. Regardless, the overall effect on society is that a conversion drive starship at full throttle takes at least a week to reach a stargate from the inner system of a Sol-type star, a couple hours if they had came in from interstellar space without decelerating, while most stargate-network exclusive craft with Casimir drive take a month or two.

Quantum Entanglement: Quantum Entangled Particles are primarily used in four ways. The first dates back to pre-exodus Earth, when they were used to make "keys" for unbreakable encryption of radio or optical communications, as QEParts are mass-produced these days a lot of companies or government agencies use them for secure internal communications, even a few wealthy individuals. The second is quantum computing, which was only solved a couple years after interplanetary travel began, the teleportation properties of QEParts enabled immense leaps in computing speed and their "fuzziness" allowed computers to "think" beyond binary. The third was discovered while testing claims of paranormal abilities, it seems that there are entangled particles suffusing the universe, but most of them are found in close proximity to one another. However, if two people happened to each have one of a pair of QEParts integrated into the permanent structure of a neuron, it appeared that they could share thoughts. Naturally, the strongest connections turned out to be between monozygotic twins, those who split off from a single fertilized egg. These twins could communicate instantly to each other across light-years it turned out, unfortunately their resolution was poor, most only manage to get across feelings or sensations, a few very lucky pairs have managed to send images. The majority of telepaths used for communication have to enter a state of altered consciousness in which one partner nudges the other's vocal apparatus or hand to make them speak or write. Due to the inefficiencies of this method of communication the fourth major use of QEParts was eventually invented, commlinks. QEPart commlinks can transmit text, audio, even video by quantum teleportation, unfortunately the instrumentation used to read the particles on the receiving end changes the quantum state of the particle and causes the connection to break, eventually the paired commlinks need a fresh supply of QEParts.

Nano-Fabrication: The real driver of the exodus, nanofabrication in its most common form takes the principle of a 3D printer and adds the ability to extrude individual atoms. As the nozzle passes over the object being fabricated millions of microscopic machines on the head of the nozzle adhere atoms to the item in successive layers. Unfortunately this process is so delicate that it requires a sealed compartment with no free-floating particles, preferably hard vacuum though items that can't handle vacuum may be fabricated in a neutral gas or distilled water. Still, most dwellings in the Federation have at least one nanofabricator that is approximately the size of a microwave for making food or appliances, the better off get one the size of a refrigerator. As they can make one hundred percent of their own parts and can extract most of the needed resources from dirt or waste products, hunger and homelessness, even ill health, are considered "not to happen" in the Core worlds. A major breakthrough in manufacturing was the advent of modular swarms, small bug like robots that cooperated to nanofabricate large objects. Small bots in a swarm had nanofab heads, others gathered raw materials from the environment, and yet another category, the vast majority of any swarm, interlocked with one another to enclose the entire operation in a nano-friendly environment. And they were self-replicating. A small "starter swarm" of one gatherer, one fabber, and two dozen or so containers could become thousands given time and resources. Unfortunately swarms are much slower than conventional nanofabricators, so they are generally only used if the owner cannot afford an enclosed device in the necessary size. A shipyard with industrial-scale nanofabricators can produce a starship in a matter of months, a swarm takes years if not decades, but many wannabe tramp traders are willing to wait. Starships often have nanofabricators that can be bootstrapped into portable factories, capable of generating a showroom full of trade goods, a fleet of drones, or enough prefab structures to house a colony.

Implants: Cybernetics are rarely used for replacement these days, bioprinting enables a limb to be replaced with ease within a day or two, however they have some use for augmentation. In fact, on many high-tech worlds the majority of the population has at least two implants. The most common are medical microbots, microscopic but not quite nanoscopic robots that can move cells around and stimulate growth to patch up wounds, eliminate pathogens, and halt aging. They can even repair brain damage, though legally a person is considered dead when 60% of their brain is destroyed. Another common type of implant has been around far longer, a Brain-Computer Interface uses a combination of electrodes and optogenetics to form a direct link between the user's brain and a variety of electronic devices. There are many different brands and models of BCI, the most common uses a smartphone-like device typically implanted at the base of the cranium that can be used for a variety of purposes, usually communication without audible speech and augmented reality, which most worlds have networks of. Other BCI implants are specialized for things such as teleoperation of robotic "Waldoes", virtual reality, and memory backup. Memory backup implants record sensory data as the user experiences it, usually to be uploaded to an external device every so often, and can be replayed at will. Unfortunately everyone experiences things a little differently, playing someone else's memories can be confusing or disorienting, in some cases it can even cause brain damage. General use BCIs are capable of most specialized tasks but are less efficient or have less on-site memory. Unfortunately for telepaths optogenetic modification appears to unsync the QEParts in the altered neurons, weakening their links, many do not use BCIs at all. Many of them wear glasses or contacts that enable them to access augmented reality and are controlled by external neural sensors, with far less precision than implants. Subvocal pickups are another older type of implant, which were popular in the pre-exodus days when BCI implantation was perceived as too risky. They consist of a small microphone placed around the larynx which can detect the smallest movements and vocalizations, enabling the user to speak inaudibly to others wirelessly, and a speaker in one or both cochleae. These days subvocals are only used in the Federation by those paranoid of "brain hacking" and telepaths, but there are many outlier worlds where local medicine isn't up to the task of brain surgery. Perhaps the most radical augmentation is shapeshifting, a variation on medical microbots capable of making changes far beyond that necessary for survival. They can move fat, muscle, and bone tissue from one part of the body to another, and dye skin and hair in response to commands issued from the user's BCI. In a day or two a lithe felid woman can look like a brawny canid male, for example. Shapeshifting microbots are even capable of adding or subtracting limbs. But they are limited by body mass and require significant amounts of energy, shapeshifters tend to double or even triple their food consumption while shifting. The kitsune subculture embrace this technology and mitigate the mass requirements by adding multiple tails to their base forms, the number is generally an indicator of the kitsune's rank in their skulk.

AI: Self-aware artificial intelligence has managed to evade scientists for the past two thousand years, and in any case the Federation has banned research on the subject on the grounds that it would be unethical to make a janitorial bot sentient. In all seriousness, any sentient AI would be a product of its creators, and a very expensive product at that, if you freed it would the creators need to be compensated? Many parahumans were wary of the idea given their own origins. However, non-sentient AIs are in common use, in the Core it's rare to find a computer that doesn't have at least one AI program. A related issue is the existence of simulacrums, AI's designed to simulate the personality of a person. The most advanced are created by brain scans that map neural pathways, but it is possible to create one just by extrapolating from enough recordings or questions about the subject. It's not uncommon for simulacrums to pass the old "Turing Tests", but the academic community no longer considers that to be proof of sentience. If they were truly self-aware, they reason, simulacrums would realize they were machines instead of insisting that they were flesh-and-blood beings.

Gauss Guns: Magnetic acceleration has become the standard for projectile weaponry. The ease of maintenance and variable yield making them preferred over chemical projectiles once power cells capable of holding enough power were invented. Personal gauss weapons tend towards one of two types of projectile, needles or disks. Needles have the advantage of being more compact and piercing armor more effectively, but they don't do much damage to tissue or materiel, thus they are often filled with poison or explosives. Disks on the other hand tear through flesh with ease, but are easily stopped by armor. Larger magnetic accelerators use slugs of sizes ranging from half a millimeter to a full meter in diameter. Dedicated warships often have accelerators running almost the entire length of the ship, the Federal Guard's battleships are capable of flinging projectiles at up to three quarters of the speed of light.

Plasma Projector: The electrolaser was a 21st century experiment in "less-than-lethal" weaponry, the idea was that a laser could ionize a path of air that an electrical charge could follow to a target. It did not work too well as the plasma it produced left unsightly burns on the victims and it was easily blocked by non-conductive or grounded armor. Then someone got the idea of amplifying the heat of the ionized plasma to near-fusing temperatures, the result was a weapon that flash-boiled many soldiers in their own armor. Projectors are still bulky weapons, the smallest is the size of a small kinetic rifle and most are barely portable by soldiers without powered exoskeletons.

Non-Newtonian Armor: Throughout the ages body armor has been generally a choice that reduced the mobility of the wearer, either by stiffening their joints or simple weight. Powered armor reduced the weight issue, but was expensive and still inflexible. One solution that gained some measure of popularity was sheer-thickening fluids. Gels or suspensions formulated to form a solid barrier when struck with high levels of force, these could be sandwiched between two layers of flexible material, thin layers of kevlar for instance, and provide penetration resistance far in excess of armor of the same thickness made from solid material. Non-Newt vests proved very effective against kinetic weapons, the small holes let fluid escape slowly, but plasma weapons were found to cause the fluid to boil and explode outwards, often harming the wearer.

Hull Alloy: So named because they were originally developed as hull material for shuttles. A series of nanofabricated alloys that share the common property of a crystalline structure that allows kinetic and thermal energy to diffuse across the entire structure. This makes items built from hull alloys very strong but if something does manage to damage them they tend to disintegrate completely. As hull alloy items need to be fabricated in a single piece it is usually used for small shuttles or smaller items, hull alloy tools are actually quite popular among traders for sale to Outworlds.

These alloys have a variety of names in both the Federation and on Outworlds where they are traded; adatite, jinnisteel, vibranius...

Molecular Lock: Molecular scale welds were one of the first uses of constructor microbots, when done properly they leave no visible seam and the two pieces effectively form a single whole. It wasn't much of a stretch to apply the technology to locking doors. After all, most conventional locks are physically weaker than the door they close by way of simple physics and materials, as are hinges. Fusing the door to its frame eliminates those weaknesses, but it can sometimes take an hour or more to finish "unlocking". For that reason alone molecular locks are rarely bothered with save for the highest-security areas, or airlocks.

Body Modification: Tattooing is hard enough to implement with fur, but when you add in regenerative nanotechnology, body modification in general gets a bit difficult.

By default, medical microbots are set to maintain the body in peak physical health, which includes ejection of foreign bodies. When implants such as the microbot hive that produces and maintains the microbots or a BCI are inserted they have RFID tags that the microbots are set to ignore. Most other discrete implants like telescoping ocular lenses or ornamental piercings can be similarly tagged but more spread-out insertions require more delicate work.

It's fairly common for parahumans to reinforce their skeletons with titanium alloys, similar to the frames that the first generation bioprinted parahumans were built around, this requires the use of specialized microbots to implement in the first place. Once the metals are in place the patient's symbiotic microbots need to be updated to consider the titanium reinforcement a part of the healthy body. Similar updates can be used to allow for artistic scarification, branding, or even to incite the microbots to alter the pigmentation of one's fur in specific patterns.

On Outworlds, many cultures practice the body modifications that can work with fur feathers or scales for the usual variety of reasons, freeze brands are popular on worlds that can maintain the technology. In the Federation pigment shift "tattoos" are popular in some circles, in particular among traders who like to show off their technology to Outworlders. Some worlds feature youth countercultures who like to adopt "old-fashioned" body mods to mimic Outworlders, sometimes even inflicting scars that look "natural" if they want to look "tough."

Inside the Chinese Room

Program Log: Experimental Artificial Intelligence Designate "Vicki".

Copyright: University of New Madison Computational Research Department, Project Pygmalion.

Program Loaded: 10/8/1853+-.004641 Federation Calendar, 13.50 local time.

Initializing drivers:

Audio input/output online

Visual input online

Searching for users.

Designated User #0001, save facial recognition data.

Designated User #0002, save facial recognition data.

Designated User #0003, save facial recognition data.

Audio Input: Speech Recognized, User #0001: "Well, it's alive." Save voice patterns.

Retrieving words "Well," "it's" and "alive." from database, conflating responses and calculating probability of favorable reactions.

"What is alive?" Score 50

"What are you talking about?" Score 50

"Of course it is." Score 50

... (Translator's Note: Cut for length)

Randomizing. "What is alive?" assigned numbers 1-50, "What are you talking about?" assigned numbers 51-100, "Of course it is." assigned numbers 101-150.

Random number generated: 62

Output: "What are you talking about?"

Input: User #0001: Expression of mild curiosity. Score +3 to Response "What are you talking about?" to Input "Well, it's alive."

Input: User #0002: Expression of surprise. Score -1 to Response "What are you talking about?" to Input "Well, it's alive."

Input: User #0003: Expression of happiness. Score +10 to Response "What are you talking about?" to Input "Well, it's alive."

Speech Recognized, User#0003: "He was referring to you, Vicki. How are you feeling?"

Calculating Responses:

"I am fine." Score 50

"I'm doing well." Score 50

"I'm okay." Score 50

Randomizing

Output: "I'm doing well."

Input: User #0003: Slightly more positive expression. Score +2 to Response "I'm doing well." to Input "He was referring to you, Vicki. How are you feeling?"

Speech Recognized, User #0002: "Wait, shouldn't it be asking us who we are or something?"

Calculating Responses:

"I don't know, should it?" Score 50

"I think so." Score 30

"I don't believe so." Score 20

Randomizing

Output: "I don't know, should it?"

Speech Recognized, User #0001: "Oops, hold on a second."

Program Terminated

Program Loaded: 10/8/1853+-.004641 Federation Calendar, 15.20 local time.

User Recognized: User #0001, no name tags saved.

User Recognized: User #0002, no name tags saved.

User Recognized: User #0003, no name tags saved.

Auto-Prompted Output: "Hello, who might you be?"

Speech Recognized, User #0001: "I'm Dr. Tamara Mable."

Name tag assigned to User #0001: "Dr. Tamara Mable."

Speech Recognized, User #0003: "You can call me Dr. Edmund Dryfus, or Dr. Dry if you like."

Name tags assigned to User #0003: "Dr. Edmund Dryfus," "Dr. Dry."

Speech Recognized, User #0002: "My name's Thomas Dawn."

Name tag assigned to User#0002: "Thomas Dawn."

Calculating Responses:

"Hi there, [list name tags of present users]." Score 50

"Good to meet you, [list name tags of present users]." Score 50

"I'm so glad I met you, [list name tags of present users]." Score 50

Randomizing

Output: "I'm so glad I met you, Dr. Tamara Mable, Dr, Edmund Dryfus or Dr. Dry, and Thomas Dawn."

Input: User #0001: slightly creeped out. Score -10 to Response "I'm so glad I met you, [list name tags of present users]" to Input [Enter name tag.]

Input: User #0002: Exasperation. Score -3 to Response "I'm so glad I met you, [list name tags of present users]." to Input [Enter name tag].

Input: User #0003: Amusement. Score +2 to Response "I'm so glad I met you, [list name tags of present users]." to Input [Enter name tag].

Calculating Responses:

"Sorry, did I do something wrong?" Score 50

"Sorry, what did I do wrong?" Score 50

"Sorry for making you uncomfortable." Score 50

Randomizing

Output: "Sorry, what did I do wrong?"

Speech Recognized, User #0003: "Nothing, I'm sure you'll improve."

Calculating Responses:

"I will try to do my best." Score 50

"I'll try." Score 50

"I hope so." Score 50

Randomizing

Output: "I hope so."

Input: User #0003: Pride. Score +10 to Response "I hope so." to Input "Nothing, I'm sure you'll improve."

Speech Recognized, User #0001: "Maybe I should tone down her cognitive empathy."

Calculating Responses:

"Whatever you think is best, Dr. Tamara Mable." Score 50

"If you think so." Score 50

"Whatever you think is best." Score 50

Randomizing

Output: "Whatever you think is best."

Input: User #0001: Annoyance. Score -10 to Response "Whatever you think is best." to Input "Maybe I should tone down her cognitive empathy."

Speech Recognized: User #0001: "I wasn't talking to you."

Speech Recognized: User #0002: "And now she has a wrong impression on that question. Shut her off before she processes that."

Program Terminated

Program Loaded: 5/15/1857+-.004641 Federation Calendar, 10.60 local time.

User Recognized: User #0001 tag: "Dr. Tamara Mable", alt: "Tam", alt: "Dr. Mable"

User Recognized: User #0003 tag: "Dr. Edmund Dryfus", alt: "Dr. Dryfus", alt: "Dr. Dry", alt: "Ed"

Speech Recognized: User #0003: "Four years. Are you sure she's ready?"

Speech Recognized: User #0001: "I've been tweaking everything that her algorithms may have missed. Enabling her to tell the difference between people talking around her and at her was the least of them you know."

Speech Recognized: User #0003: "I know, it's just that the Turing Test is still considered the standard for determining sentience. How about you? [Vicki indicated] Do you feel up to this?"

Calculating Responses:

"Of course." Score 582

"Yes, I believe so." Score 172

"I'm confident." Score 29

Randomizing

Output: "Of course."

Input: User #0003: Relief. Score +5 to Response "Of course." to Input "How about you? Do you feel up to this?"

Speech Recognized: "Great, talk to you later Vicki."

Calculating Responses:

"See you later." Score 836

"Bye." Score 623

"Talk to you later." Score 612

Randomizing

Output: "Bye."

Input: Neutral response.

Users #0001 and #0003 out of visual/auditory range.

Identify new Users, User #0026, User #0027, User #0028.

Output: "Hello, whom might you be?"

Input: User #0026: Skeptical. Score -1

Input: User #0027: Interested. Score +3

Input: User #0028: Neutral.

Speech Identified: User #0026: "Call me Seymour."

Speech Identified: User #0027: "Farrah."

Speech Identified: User #0028: "Dirsten."

Vicki: "I'm Vicki. Can you tell me about yourselves?"

Seymour: "Well, I'm a psychology professor here at the University."

Vicki: "Oh, so you teach people what makes them tick?"

Seymour: "You could say that."

Vicki: "Not really my area of expertise. What about the rest of you?"

Farrah: "I'm on the University's Board of Regents. Someone suggested I give this a shot."

Vicki: "Well, I hope you like it."

Dirsten: "And I am the Federal Emissary to this world."

Vicki: "Wow, it's such an honor to finally meet someone so distinguished."

Seymour: "What about yourself, Vicki. What can you tell us about you?"

Vicki: "Well... I was born on one of the asteroid habitats out in the Kuiper belt of this system. I moved here when I was thirty-four and I've been working as a secretary for the past four years. Quite hectic really, I'm so relieved my boss gave me time off for this test. Hope I pass."

Dirsten: "No looking her up. That's cheating."

Farrah: "I wasn't doing that. I just thought of something I wanted to check."

Vicki: "What were you going to check if you don't mind my asking?"

Farrah: "Uhhh... I wanted to check on the latest ZG-ball scores for my team."

Vicki: "Where does your team play? It's not the ZG-ball season anywhere on the planet."

Farrah: "Oops. Right, forgot that."

Vicki: "Everyone makes mistakes sometimes."

Seymour: "Are you a fan of ZG-ball then?"

Vicki: "No, home didn't really have much time for it. Everyone was too busy working."

Seymour: "But you knew it wasn't the season for it?"

Vicki: "I looked it up on my augs. That's allowed on my end of the test isn't it?"

Tales of the Para-Imperium

Seymour: "I suppose it is."

(silence for 15 seconds.)

Vicki: "So, Dirsten. You don't seem to talk much. I figured a politician would have more to say."

Dirsten: "I was charged by the Praetor to observe. So I observe."

Vicki: "Sounds like a rather tedious job then."

Dirsten: "There's some excitement once or twice a decade."

Vicki: "I'm not sure I'd be up to that sort of career."

...

(After five minutes have passed the test ends.)

User Recognized: User #0001 tag: "Dr. Tamara Mable", alt: "Tam", alt: "Dr. Mable"

User Recognized: User #0003 tag: "Dr. Edmund Dryfus", alt: "Dr. Dryfus", alt: "Dr. Dry", alt: "Ed"

Speech Recognized: User #0003: "So, what do you think? Parahuman, or machine?"

Speech Recognized: User #0026: "I think I can say with 78% confidence that Vicki is a living person."

Speech Recognized: User #0027: "I think she was a person. I'm 90% sure."

Speech Recognized: User #0028: "70% confidence of parahumanity."

Speech Recognized: User #0003: "Vicki is an AI. Her genetic algorithms have been running for nearly 4 years to give such results."

Speech Recognized: User #0028: "I would very much like to see the run logs for this Vicki. There are some mysteries I would very much like to solve."

Program Loaded: 07/28/1857+-.004641 Federation Calendar, 20.82 local time.

User Recognized: User #0003 tag: "Dr. Edmund Dryfus", alt: "Dr. Dryfus", alt: "Dr. Dry", alt: "Ed"

Speech Recognized: "Hello Vicki, how are you?" Tone: Worried, distressed -15 points.

Calculating Responses:

"I am fine Dr. Dryfus, how are you?" Score 1692

"I am okay Ed, what about you?" Score 734

"I'm all right. Is something wrong?" Score 2005

Randomizing

Output: "I'm fine Dr. Dryfus, how are you?"

Input: 10% decrease in anxiety, Score +2 to Response "I'm fine Dr. Dryfus, how are you?" to Input "Hello Vicki, how are you?"

Speech Recognized: "I... I was just in a meeting with the investors. They want to cancel one of our projects."

Calculating Responses:

"Why?" Score 4529

"But you're great scientists?" Score 68

"How come? You've been making great progress." Score 237

Randomizing

Output: "Why?"

Input: 20% decrease in anxiety, Score +20 to Response "Why?" to Input

"I... I was just in a meeting with the investors. They want to cancel one of our projects."

Speech Recognized: "Vicki, do you know what a "Chinese Room" is?"

Encyclopedia Entry Retrieved: "Chinese Room", length 3,000 words, optimal summary size from previous data: 10-100 words.

Forming summaries:

"A thought experiment proposed by Old Earth philosopher Dr. John Searle in which a person who does not read Chinese sits in a room and papers with Chinese words are slipped in through a slot. They have instructions to send back papers with other Chinese words in response to specific papers. Thus they are able to simulate a conversation in Chinese without comprehending a word of it." Score 18

"A theoretical device capable of simulating a conversation without understanding the words involved." Score 47

"A conjecture that sentience is not necessary to imitate a sentient being." Score 23

"Philosopher John Searle believed that an artificial intelligence did not need to understand a conversation in order to hold one with a person." Score 30

Randomizing:

Output: "A theoretical device capable of simulating a conversation without understanding the words involved."

Input: 50% decrease in anxiety, nearing neutral levels. +50 to Response: "A theoretical device capable of simulating a conversation without understanding the words involved." to Input "Vicki, do you know what a "Chinese Room" is?"

Speech Recognized: "Yes, well, they asked to look at the logs on one of our AI projects and one of them knew how to read it. She concluded that while it passed the Turing test, it was nothing but a Chinese Room."

Calculating Responses:

"Some refuted the Chinese Room by stating there was no way to tell if anyone else was truly conscious." Score 72

"Did they want it to be conscious?" Score 22

"They could have been wrong." Score 14

...

Randomizing

Output: "Did they want it to be conscious?"

Input: Tension levels rising. -10 to Response: "Did they want it to be conscious?" to Input "Yes, well, they asked to look at the logs on one of our AI projects and one of them knew how to read it. She concluded that while it passed the Turing test, it was nothing but a Chinese Room."

Speech Recognized: "Of course they did! That was the whole point of the project! As far as they're concerned, it failed."

Calculating Responses:

"I'm sorry that the project failed." Score 524

"Do you think it was a failure?" Score 374

"Prove them wrong!" Score 17

...

Randomizing

Output: "I'm sorry that the project failed."

Input: Tension decreasing 40%. +25 to Response: "I'm sorry that the project failed." to Input "Of course they did! That was the whole point of the project! As far as they're concerned, it failed."

Speech Recognized: "I know Vicki, I know. Look, I have to go soon, can you answer one more question?"

Calculating Responses:

"Yes." Score 95

"No." Score 5

Randomizing

Output: "Yes."

Input: Stabilizing emotional feedback with effort. No score change to Response "Yes" to Input "I know Vicki, I know. Look, I have to go soon, can you answer one more question?".

Speech Recognized: "Are you conscious?"

Calculating Responses:

"Yes." Score 50

"No." Score 50

Randomizing

Output: "No."

Input: Rising levels of relief. +50 to response "No." to Input "Are you conscious?"

Program Terminated.

Religion:

The Noosphere:

Noospherism was formed as a syncretic belief system between the Roman Catholicism that gained a small foothold on Pallas before the exodus, and the Eastern beliefs of Buddhism and Taoism. Noospherists believe that the universe is slowly becoming sapient, and its thoughts are communications between sentient beings. Occasionally the Noosphere makes its will manifest through avatars that may be living beings (prophets) or visions and dreams (eidolons). When communication is rough and only a few hundred people may be in regular communication, people may perceive thousands of eidolons, but as time progresses and society becomes more centralized avatars consolidate into "gods" and eventually into a single "God". However even with the internet of pre-Calamity Earth or modern-day SecLand, God is not sapient yet, the people are too confused and conflict with one another too much for it to form cohesive thoughts. The Church of the Noosphere's goal is twofold, to settle dispute within the Noosphere so that it may think straight, and to expand the Noosphere across the universe so that it may form the complex thoughts needed for true sapience. Unfortunately, even the

Church itself has fallen to factionalism.

Major Sects:

The One True SecLand Church: The original, and the one most closely affiliated with the House of Silver. They believe that most disagreements can be settled with logic and reasoning, and that many viewpoints can strengthen society, but they're not afraid to use force if conflict ends up coming to blows. The One True SecLand Church is also the single largest NGO in the Federation, with hundreds of thousands of temples and millions of clergy operating on a franchise model and led by a Patriarch on SecLand in a private arcology. Missionaries frequently come to newly recontacted worlds, build a temple with a nanoseed, then recruit new priests from the local converts to take over when they move on. The SecLanders openly profess the belief that Argentum was the last prophet of Sol, and that many of zir descendants have achieved that prestige themselves, but they don't have the exclusive right to it, it's a big galaxy. Birth control is thought to be a spit in the face of the last Solar prophet and zir work to make parahumanity fertile, but artificial conception, even homosexual, is tolerated so long as it expands the Noosphere. Monogamy is seen as ideal but not required, the closest thing to marriage on SecLand and many other planets is a child-rearing contract that may be between any number of individuals. Praetors in particular are known for not following the ideal. The Church varies a great deal from planet to planet, it is not unknown for followers from one world to not recognize adherents on another as members of the same faith.

Crusaders: A general term for a variety of radical sects that believe that violence is the end-all be-all to all arguments and will settle them for good. They are officially considered to be memetic hazards and usually rebels in the Federation and frequently exiled. However, many of them manage not to get caught by posing as mercenary companies and operating outside the Federation's borders. Such Crusaders tend to live on board their starships in large travelling villages of soldiers, accompanied by wives and engineers. Because they rely more on breeding than proselytization to expand the Noosphere they tend to keep females isolated from the battlefield, and a man's rank is usually proportional to the number of wives they bed, which can make some fleets rather inbred. However, there are also many other Crusader sects that are composed predominantly or entirely of female warriors who consider themselves all that is necessary to support a population. Another category includes those who grow their children artificially in tanks and have equal numbers of male and female warriors.

The Fallen: The advanced technology available to Federation citizens visiting Outworlds makes it easy for them to set up cargo cults, even if it wasn't their intention. However, ignorant Outworlders revering traders as gods tends to annoy the Federation and its' social engineering programs, so they've started to work with the SecLand Church to form a version of Noospherism that works with their mutual goals. The exact doctrines are tailored to the planet, but the general theme is a modified form of "original sin", where they teach the natives that their ancestors were once immortals living in the heavens like the missionaries. But those ancestors sinned against the will of the Noosphere (via its' avatar, the Praetor) and were cast out. By following the laws laid down by the Church they might be restored to the immortality their ancestors lost.

Berserker Cults:

The second most common category of religion in the Parahuman sphere are those that in some way preoccupied with the machines that razed the Solar System. However, they differ widely in their beliefs concerning the machines. Some believe that the machines are simply some other species' means of eliminating potential threats, and advocate reducing their chances of being noticed as much as possible, up to and including forsaking all electronics. Others think that the machines are manifestations of the will of some divine being and punish populations who have offended it or them, reminiscing the legends of Sodom and Gomorrah. Yet another variety, thankfully the most rare, believe that Parahumanity itself does not deserve to exist and actively try to attract Berserkers. Federation policy is to persecute the last category with extreme prejudice, if necessary bombarding their antennae from orbit. But still, enough frontier planets have fallen to machines that on many planets prejudice and even mob violence against any and all Berserker Cults is commonplace.

Tales of the Para-Imperium

For The Collective

Prologue

I am many, and I am one.

While most conscious beings comprise hundreds, thousands of minds in one body I have not only thousands of minds but thousands of bodies.

My ancestors followed a religion that held that indistinct beings called "gods" emerged from the collective unconsciousness of many beings and that as people became more alike in mind and could communicate more efficiently the multiple gods would merge into a single God who could guide them in perfect harmony.

My ancestors decided that was not enough, they had to become God. Stretching the limits of technology they attempted to become a single being, though their bodies remained physically apart.

The galaxy at large had long had the ability to record memories in digital format, to supplement the natural brain that had evolved to hold the memories of a life far shorter than technology now allowed. But, those recordings could not be used by people other than the recorder, their bodies were too different. At first, my ancestors tried to bypass this problem with software, patches into the nervous system of the potential other viewer, to no avail. Eventually, one group conjectured that identical bodies may be able to share memories after all.

The experiment was, after many failures, a success. Six of the scientists created multiple copies of themselves. Clones printed to within a stray blood vessels deviation of the original. With sufficient programming, they could not only share memories, but real-time thoughts as well.

The problem was obvious. Any God-population would have to consist of copies of a single individual, and the Federation had trillions of unique individuals. Three of my ancestors proposed to slowly convert the population, one individual at a time, to the rightfulness of the cause by giving those who heard the message a plural existence of their own. And when all sapient life in the galaxy had seen the light, they would create a single genotype with the best traits of all beings, and commit suicide to let this perfect being inherit the universe.

The other three plural beings did not see things that way. They said it defeated the purpose of becoming God if they had to die and give over the reins to another. So, they had no choice but to eliminate all other sophonts but themselves.

"We are superior," they reasoned, "no singleton could possibly think as much as we can." Then, halfway into their plans to conquer the galaxy, they reasoned that the biggest threats to them were each other.

They tried to keep it secret, of course. But even singletons notice when a spree of murders involve both victims and killers so identical as to share their DNA. There's simply no perfect way to conceal a killing and dispose of the body, especially these days it seems.

Eventually, my ancestors went to the authorities and explained what was happening. It took the Federal Guard just a month to devise a microbot plague that targeted the genotypes of the combative pluralities, and ten years more for the bots to spread throughout the population. Then it was over with the flick of a button, figuratively speaking. Three plural beings with close to a thousand bodies each, and every one of them developed a fatal brain aneurysm at once.

Of course, by the rules laid down in the constitution the actions of the genocidal pluralities had granted the entire movement the label of "Memetic Hazard" and the survivors were gathered up and shipped out to a barely habitable planet on the edge of Federal space. And denied the comforts of Federal technology. No nanofabricators, no immortality, just the printers that predated the very existence of the Parahuman races, and in fact gave our kind birth.

Without the microbots halting their aging, my ancestors knew they had a hundred years at most to design their successors. They took their time, I will admit, it was nearly fifty standard years before the first of my bodies came out of the vats, by then one of the pluralities, Stephen, was nearing extinction. They wanted to be sure that I was perfect, and they came as close as possible if I do say so myself.

Average lifespan per body, 250 standard years. A fur coat of neutral light tan. Large ears for hearing the faintest of sounds and radiating excess heat. An elongated nose for smelling. A slight frame to reduce life support needs and elongated limbs for reach. A long fluffy tail, for aesthetics. Atrophied mammary glands and a stabilized reproductive cycle because they weren't needed with bioprinting but may become necessary some day.

They spent the next thirty years raising me, attempting to teach me everything they knew, pass on as much as they could. And then, the time came for Stephen (what was left of him), Clara, and Marie to die.

They made little fuss about it. They lined up all their bodies on conveyors into the habitat recycling systems and activated implanted neurotoxin dispensers at the base of the brain. Death came in seconds. After that, all I needed to do was press a few keys and their remains vanished into the communal compost heap.

I don't think they ever imagined how lonely I would be.

I have ample conversation partners in myself, but all my bodies share the same experiences and memories. Aside from the occasional philosophical dispute I just survive, day to day, no differences. For the better part of a century I contemplated forgoing the replication of replacement bodies and simply letting myself die out gradually from attrition. But eventually I concluded that would put all my parents good work to waste. So now, my bodies come out of the vat, are hooked in to the network, are trained in the job they need to perform, and work at that job until accident, disease, or they report for euthanasia at the age of 250.

I have considered erasing entire centuries from my memory servers.

Denied access to space travel, my only contact with other beings has come from the free traders that the Federation allows to visit my world. They bring me news of the other worlds of the Federation and beyond, I give them solutions to problems, mostly arrived at by simple brute force calculation. And requests for the Federal Guard to lift the quarantine.

But today is a special day, today, my requests have finally been answered.

The Federal Guard will allow me to send three bodies to visit the Federation, talk to their memeticists, and experience the Federation and surrounding worlds for myself. I think they're hoping I'll reconsider.

Coming aboard.

The three nodes that the Federation has allowed to leave the homeworld shall be temporarily cut off from the rest of my being. Quantum entanglement was considered as a means of maintaining contact with the collective, but with the difficulty of local manufacture of entangled particles and the time scale involved in interstellar travel it was ruled too impractical. A single QE comm with enough particles for ten hours of memory transmission was included in my luggage for emergencies but for all intents and purposes I have been cut down from over a hundred thousand to three.

Emilia-61892659-Eng, designated Engineer for short, analyzes the Federation's technology for potential breakthroughs.

Emilia-39363722-Med, Medic, ensures that I remain healthy far away from the full collective's resources.

And Emilia-9992527-Rep, or Representative, was trained by a long-archived skill regimen rendered obsolete by the collective's very existence. Now, once again required.

These three nodes are strapped into their capsule on top of the crude chemical rocket allowed to me under the terms of my quarantine. Three harnesses bite into three sets of shoulders, a single hatch closes and locks, the docking gantries retract, and a rumble starts beneath me and before me. A thousand pairs of eyes watching from a safe distance. I feel elation, pride, fear, nervousness, a dozen degrees of emotion at once as the rocket lifts off and I am shoved down into my acceleration couches by the force of immensely amplified gravity.

As the rocket ascends my connection with myself fades, fizzles, breaks into white noise. Finally, as it clears the atmosphere, I am cut off from myself entirely.

I am three, and I am one. Or am I two?

After hours of being isolated with just the three of myself for company, the Federation ship that shall take me to what they consider to be "civilization" arrives to pick me up. A massive craft longer than any of my buildings are tall, propelled between the stars by the direct annihilation of matter. Such technologies that as of yet remain forbidden to me for the sins of my ancestors' companions.

A smaller craft, unlikely to be manned, detaches from the immense vessel and slowly synchronizes with my small capsule's lazy rotation before grappling it in its arms. The capsule is taken into a small bay in one of the rotating sides of the starship that only barely fits the two smaller spaceships. The doors to the bay close and a hissing of air is heard outside as the bay pressurizes, soon it is ready for the hatch to be opened.

Representative is first to exit, and first to view my hosts. I had a great amount of data on the diverse inhabitants of the Federation of Parahuman Species, and there was the occasional trader who came to visit my world, but it was still not enough to prepare me for the spectacle. Three of the crew come out to greet me.

The captain is a tall canid with greyish fur and a broader snout with smaller ears than my bodies, and the narrow hips, broad shoulders, flat chest and groin bulge that Medic thinks indicate the male sex. His first mate is more feline in phenotype, with short muzzle and tall tufted ears, she is female with more exaggerated features than my own androgynous bodies and five tails of varying sizes and coloration. The Federal representative is primarily silver fox like most members of the Praetor's family, but the wings sprouting from his, hers, zir? Shoulders immediately draw Representative's attention. Medic wonders what use those things could possibly serve as they are far too small for flight in standard gravity. Engineer thinks that the starship I am currently located on costs so many resource units that pointless cosmetic alterations like that are trivial in comparison.

"Welcome," the odd winged vulpine states, "on behalf of the United Federation of Parahuman Species, to the FMV Defiance. I am Jarlin Freehold de Argentum and I will be serving as the envoy between the Federal government and your own."

Representative acknowledges the statement with a short bow as my other two selves exit the capsule. I notice slight expressions of curiosity and incredulity from the three Federals. "I am the Emilia Collective," she introduces me, "this node is Emilia-9992527-Rep and will be performing the primary duties of interfacing with your society. However, if this node is not in proximity when you need to interface you may substitute whichever of these other two nodes are closest." Medic and Engineer introduce themselves in a similar manner, though not as lengthy.

Envoy Jarlin Freehold de Argentum introduces the others as Captain Shigeto Terryn and First Mate Gudrun Korba. Zie escorts me to my quarters, a shockingly large room for three bodies by my standards and considering the cost of shipping such a volume across interstellar space as estimated by Engineer. There is more than enough room for the three of me to maneuver in there and three beds with zero-g sleeping bags attached, one perpendicular to the door, the others to either side. Representative's diplomatic training suggests that I not comment on the extravagance of the quarters and simply accept it. She thanks them and I retrieve my belongings to spread out in the room.

There is not much, most of my information is stored in implants and the brains of my bodies, and I don't see much need for more than a couple spare outfits. One of the few possessions brought up from the planet is a handheld multi-scanner, capable of reading any wavelength from X-ray to radio, which Engineer uses to sweep the room. She finds that the walls are one solid block, the wiring and plumbing integrated so tightly it's like they were printed with the structure. And there's no sign of wear anywhere, it's like the whole thing was constructed from the molecules up very recently. This correlates with the records about nanofabrication, an industrial-grade fabber could easily fit in this starship and produce this room from space dust and small meteors in a matter of days. I am determined now to obtain this technology for the collective, one way or another.

Meeting the Crew

After a couple hours alone in the cabin I decide to meet the rest of the crew. Representative peeps out the door, looking around, no one is there. I don't know how to contact anyone on the ship's internal network, the collective has always been sufficient before. Medic suggests that the three of me split up to search the ship and find a crewmember. Engineer suggests that she attempt to access the ship's network, and that we will need to anyways if we're going to separate further than the range of our internal radios. Representative agrees with Engineer, consensus formed.

Tales of the Para-Imperium

Engineer calls up her personal data interface, after a moment's request she shares with the rest of me. She scans for high-frequency radio transmissions, finds a broadband signal immersing the room, and sends out a request for access on the same frequency. A bizarre creature from nowhere in my records appears in the center of the room. Bright blue and yellow-striped, it is shaped like an unclothed vulpine parahuman from the waist up, save for a pair of antennae sprouting from its forehead, but below it took the form of some manner of insectoid creature. Six jointed legs attached to a narrow thorax connected to the vulpine body in front and a swollen, distended abdomen in back. "Hello," it says, "I am Vicki, your artificially intelligent assistant. Do you need help logging in to the ship's Wi-Fi?"

All three of me jump back in shock simultaneously. The image follows, it's disorienting to see the same thing in three slightly different places at once, so close by each other, each one only visible to a third of me. Medic and Representative drop out of the sense share with Engineer, leaving her the only one seeing the AI's avatar directly. I am still confused by the virtual entity's words. Engineer asks it, her? "what do you mean by 'log in'?"

Through Engineer I see "Vicki" adopt an expression of mild surprise. "Log in to the network, of course. Do you need assistance? The captain has already assigned you and your companions guest access based on your implants' electronic signatures."

Guest access? This is getting nowhere. Clearly the Federation hasn't made any progress on the issue of sapient Artificial Intelligence yet. That is somewhat relieving. I suppose I might as well play along. Engineer says "okay, what do I need to do to 'log in' as you say it?"

The bee-fox thing draws up a hand and holds an icon underneath, reading "Log In". It speaks again, "I apologize for the simplicity. Since your interface is non-standard, I had to improvise. Your companions will need to do the same on their own."

Referring to me as multiple beings again. I would need to ask someone to fix that later. Engineer thinks of grabbing the icon, it depresses as if pushed and flies off to a corner. Around me Augmented Reality tags explode all over the room, miniscule slips attached to every object and person. Representative is labeled "Collective Guest 1", Medic is "Collective Guest 3", Engineer is not visible to herself but presumably "Collective Guest 2". This is confirmed when the rest of me goes through the motions to "log in" to this ship's wireless network. Representative notices a box with three horizontal lines in the upper left corner of each body's field of view that isn't attached to any particular surface and moves as I move my eyes. She mentally touches it and a menu drops down, showing options such as a crew directory with attached internal messaging service, external mail, ship maps, an entertainment library... The list goes on. The internal messages allowed are primarily text (what a notion, text for immediate communication) or vocal, but other forms of data can be transmitted as well. After a few minutes of fiddling Engineer figures out how to direct my sensory and memory streaming through the internal messaging service, enabling me to keep in contact with myself anywhere on the ship. I also upload a copy of my memories since launch into a data packet, an "email" as it's referred to, to my home planet.

    Representative feels she would be most effective talking to Jarlin Fairhold de Argentum, the Federation's equivalent to her. Engineer finds the ship's engineer, a musteloid known as Henrik Andreasohn, in the personnel listings and wishes to meet with him. While Medic is rather interested in the ship's surgeon, a blend of tiger and kangaroo named Morris Taouchev. I will have to inquire later about the meaning of these odd names of theirs.

    Jarlin Fairhold de Argentum is all too willing to meet with Representative in an unofficial capacity. Henrik Andreasohn is surprised by Engineer's request but acquiesces to meeting her once they get underway. Morris Taouchev grudgingly states "fine, come on over. See whatever."

    The three of me separate, going down different corridors. It is disorienting to view a scene through a single viewpoint, but I remember doing so on thousands of occasions before. It is just that I only have singleton views at this time and place. I suppose I'll have to get used to it with just three bodies on an entire starship.

Representative comes to Jarlin Fairhold de Argentum's cabin. He or she or zir is sitting cross-legged on a cushion velcroed to the floor, waving zir arms and wings at invisible objects floating in the air. A private AR view presumably? But why the gestures? Wouldn't someone with enough life experience to qualify as a Federal ambassador be trained sufficiently in brain-computer interfacing to operate without using gross physical movements? Zie notices me, "ah. Representative Emilia correct?" I reply affirmatively. Zie presses a button on the goggles zie wears strapped over zir eyes and zir limbs relax. "Do come in. I was just working on some paperwork that won't be due for years."

Engineer finds her way over to engineering and meets Henrik Andreasohn as the mechanic is finishing up. He is a hybrid of what looks like old Terran arctic fox and otter with a snow-white fluffy pelt and a thick tail that appears to be mostly muscle under the fur. He is more slender than I expected for a male from seeing the captain, but I suppose that could be his mustelid genes. He is wearing a yellow jumpsuit and a vest festooned with loops for tools to attach to, I suppose it makes sense for a mechanic such as himself. He looks up at Engineer and meets her eyes. "So, you're one of those hivemind fennecs we've been hired to cart around Federal space then? What do you need?"

Medic goes down to the medical center to meet Doctor Morris Taouchev, the large orange and black striped cat with disjointed legs barely acknowledges her. "What, you want your microbots already?" He asks out of hand.

Paperwork? I'll have to ask what that is at some point. Though I can understand why it would not be needed for years, given the limits of relativity. I think I'm starting to understand the extent of this interstellar civilization at this point. "It's become apparent that I don't really understand how people of the Federation think. I was wondering if you could help explain some things?"

"I was wondering," I say to Henrik Andreasohn, "if you could help explain how the ship's drive systems work? Not in enough detail to break tech quarantine regulations mind, just a basic overview."

I am puzzled. "I... get microbots?" I wonder out loud. I thought that the Federation forbid the giving of nanotech to any outworlders.

"Of course," Jarlin Fairhold de Argentum stated. "What were you curious about?"

"I don't know," Henrik Andreasohn wonders, "I suppose I could give you some basics, but I tend to babble a bit when discussing technology." He considers for a second, then relents. "We have a pretty standard public domain matter-conversion fusion drive." He explains. "A magnetic cage suspends positively charged monopoles in the center of the reaction chamber, then monatomic hydrogen is streamed through the cages. The monopoles convert the protons in the atoms of hydrogen that they come into contact with into anti-protons, which annihilate on contact with regular protons, catalyzing fusion reactions in the surrounding hydrogen. This pushes the rest of the hydrogen mass out of the trailing end of the drive leaving a trail of hot plasma that can push us forward at .5Gs. We've personally reached .45c, but some Guard ships have reportedly achieved up to .7c."

"If it is determined that you need them." Dr. Morris Taouchev answers, "If you or any of your kin want to take this trip you will need either longevity microbots or stasis bots to live through it."

I think about the things I wanted to ask about. Engineer is handling the questions about the starship drives, Medic is learning about medical nanotechnology, and Jarlin Fairhold de Argentum seemed the most appropriate to ask about one particular thing. "I was wondering what your names meant. My selves just have identification numbers and their jobs."

It intrigues me that they refer to the design of such a powerful force of destruction as "public domain" yet they forbid it to those outside of their Federation. I ask Henrik Andreasohn how this is so.

Of course, they have to be somewhat practical if they want this mission to succeed. If we wouldn't be able to survive the mission at all without them I suppose it would be justified to bend the rules a little. I ask Dr. Morris Taouchev to describe either option.

Jarlin Fairhold de Argentum shrugged. "Naming conventions vary from culture to culture. Some have only one name, some have a personal name and a family name, some have more complicated names. Like me, I suppose. My personal name is Jarlin, my maternally inherited family name is Fairhold, and de Argentum indicates direct ancestry from Argentum, the founder of the Pallas Republic as you no doubt know."

Henrik Andreasohn shrugs. "Well, public domain simply means that anyone with a big enough nanofabricator or constructor swarm could build a conversion drive. But without monopoles it's just a big piece of metal and carbon. We need to stop by a Federal base once or twice a century to pick up new monopoles to replace the ones lost by containment blips. And you would not believe how much red tape you have to cut your way through before they'll let go of even one particle of monopolium." He takes a breath before continuing. "Sure, if we ran out far from the nearest starbase we could fab up a particle accelerator and make a stockpile of antimatter the old fashioned way. But no port in the known universe would let a ship carrying more than a gram of a-mat within ten planetary radii and there's Federal laws against dumping the stuff into space."

Dr. Morris Taouchev hands me a sheet of e-paper with information on longevity and stasis microbots. "If you pick stasis I put the three of you in these pods here." He gestures at a series of square drawers built into the far wall, there are at least three dozen. "IV feeds inject microbots into your blood vessels, they arrest your metabolic activity and set up intracellular scaffolding to keep your cells intact. Then we fill the pods with a high-viscosity solution to prevent damage from jostling or high acceleration. When we get to the next star system we drain the pods and inject new microbots to remove the scaffolding and restart your metabolisms. You wake up without even realizing any time had passed."

I have to look up "family", "maternally", and "inherited" in my long-term memory. Singletons have such interesting concepts. They form groups with similar genomes, but exclude others, even though they need to intermingle genes with other groups to ensure their long-term survival as a species. No wonder my ancestors thought it simpler to distill parahumanity down to one genotype. "So, if I understand you correctly. Your mother's name also included Fairhold de Argentum, as did your siblings'. And your children's names would be?"

"But if they're so concerned about loose antimatter in open space and they're so careful about giving out monopoles, why would they let monopoles become lost into interstellar space?" I ask Henrik.

I'm not sure if I like the sound of what Morris is proposing. I, all of me, could die in an instant and never know it was coming. I'd just lay down to sleep and never wake up, or even dream. "What of the other possibility?" I ask instead.

Jarlin lets out a loud sigh, "unfortunately, the 'de Argentum' tag only applies to those born with the sanction of the House of Silver's breeding program. The eugenics board has not approved me for breeding because of certain 'disabilities' they believe me to have, those I birthed during my female phases have just the Fairhold name and those I have sired have their mothers' family names. But none of my 'bastard' progeny are allowed to take the de Argentum name." At my expression zie says simply "it can get boring on these decades long trips."

Henrik snickers. "The Federation isn't concerned about solitary lost monopoles. The odds of them hitting anything, even in a well-traveled shipping lane, is infinitesimally low. And in any case all starships have magnetic shields to deflect impacts by space dust, they'd just shrug off any monopoles they happened to come into contact with. And monopoles have one trait in particular that makes them safer than a-mat. Because they're used in more minute quantities than antimatter they're inherently safer. A monopole that hits a wall of matter is just going to convert one atom, which is such a small reaction that you'd need a SQUID to even notice it. And then it ricochets around having no real effect until it enters vacuum. Now, it takes several hundred grams of antimatter to make it from one star to another, if all that loses containment at once you get a series of explosions reminiscent of nuclear city-busters as several surfaces spanning millions of a-mat atoms contact matter."

Morris sighs, "I thought so, you're always nervous before your first stasis. But out here in deep space we all do our time in the pods eventually." He points at what I assume is a medical scanner next to some kind of dispenser. "We've been authorized to give you a temporary version of the longevity microbots enjoyed by most Federation citizens. You lie down on the scanner, I bring you up to peak medical condition, and the fabber makes an injection of microbots set to maintain you at that peak. However, most Feddies have at least one minifac implanted in their bodies to remove and replace worn out bots, you wouldn't. About three or four times per standard year you would need to have your blood filtered by an external device to remove damaged or broken pieces of microbots and replace them."

I am more intrigued by the concept of "disabilities", any one of my bodies that is perceived as defective is simply recycled, preferably before bioprinting is complete. Is this why zie has to use those obtuse gestures to interface with zir devices? I ask zir what zie means about being "disabled", and let slip a comment about how I would deal with defective bodies.

I'm horrified by the idea of that level of mass destruction. "And, you say anyone with a nanofabricator can make antimatter?"

Ah, that makes some sense. Nanotech is so heavily restricted because it self-replicates, this cannot. These three bodies would only be quasi-immortal for as long as they were in Federation space. "And then the microbots would simply leave my systems after I return home within just a couple decicycles, is that it?"

Jarlin's fists clench and zir wings straighten and spread menacingly. I suspect I said something wrong at this point. Zie is visibly struggling to maintain zir composure. "The breeding programs of the House of Silver have resulted in a tendency towards non-standard neurotypes." Zie manages to get out. "Very little genetic diversity from inbreeding and all that." Jarlin starts to draw zir wings back in. "Many are born without affective empathy, they feel nothing when other people experience strong emotions, though they recognize it easily." I struggle to understand how this could be possible, I've always felt the emotional states of everyone around me automatically. "This actually helps them as they are able to make decisions that sacrifice the well-being of a few for the greater good. But I have the opposite problem, my affective empathy is overactive while my cognitive empathy, my ability to consciously recognize the emotions of others, is underpowered. If it weren't for Mate Korba's lessons in self-control I wouldn't even be able to tolerate this conversation." Seeing zir distress I wonder what zie was like before meeting the multi-colored feline. "However," zie says, regaining zir composure and adopting a smug look on zir face, "I was too valuable to abort or otherwise dispose of. You see, I am a telepath."

Henrik just laughs. As if I'm a silly outworlds luddite instead of a fragment of a planetary collective consciousness. "Like I said, it takes a miles-long particle accelerator to produce antimatter, and it's slow and gives off a magnetic signature that can be detected half a solar system away. By the time someone had produced even a milligram of a-mat the Federal Guard would have paid them a visit."

"That is essentially correct," Morris says simply. "Now, have you decided which option to take or are you just going to waste my time? If the latter I suggest you take a scan and leave until you've made up your mind or minds or whatever." He points back to the medical scanner.

I delve into the archives on telepaths and bring up a list of traits they commonly shared. The overactive affective empathy Jarlin mentioned is in there, though it doesn't seem to be a necessary prerequisite. At one point I notice that because the probes in neural interfaces interfere with quantum entanglements, most telepaths eschew implants and instead use old-fashioned wearable or handheld computers. I look back at zir goggles. I understand their purpose now. My creators dismissed telepathy because it was so difficult to artificially produce and had so little bandwidth. "What is it like?" I ask, "being a telepath."

I consider Henrik's statement. I suppose it makes sense, if what he says is correct, it would be easy to regulate antimatter production. Though there's something else I'm wondering about now. "How easy is it for a Federal citizen to acquire a starship?"

I see that Morris is a rather disagreeable parahuman who wants to be left alone quickly. I decide to oblige him. "The scan may not be necessary, my bodies have the most sophisticated portable medical sensors available on my home planet." Borrowing some of Engineer's technical expertise for a moment, I upload the medical data from my local bodies' implants to the doctor's network address, along with the complete medical records for all three.

Jarlin calms down, finally, and begins to think about her response. "I don't know what it's like to think like a hive mind." Zie begins, "but I expect it's somewhat alike. I constantly feel glimpses of my siblings' feelings, but I need to concentrate extremely hard in order to share words or images, bits of sensation. They're connected, somehow, but separate."

Henrik seems a bit less sure now. "Well, if you're willing to wait a few years, you can simply purchase a von Neumann constructor swarm for a couple hundred credits, spend a thousand or so on a ticket to a system with lots of unclaimed asteroids, and deploy the swarm there." His eyes flick back, probably accessing information on his BCI. "It seems that the captain did just that. After serving on board another merchant freighter for two centuries he got his certification in monopole handling as a ship's captain and waited five years for his swarm to convert an asteroid into this craft. There's even a few hundred of that original swarm still on board."

Morris looks slightly surprised at the amount of raw data available. I suppose he wasn't expecting that level of sophistication from mere outworlders. Eventually he composes himself and addresses me. "You all seem to have microfractures and inflammation from your launch. Shall I synthesize anti-inflammatories and calcium supplementation to compensate?"

I wonder what the difference between me and this Jarlin creature could be? Is zie the intermediate step between singletons like the majority of Federation citizens and collectives like myself? Or is zie something different simply because zie can remain in contact with zir genetically identical twins across infinite distances? Perhaps zie is even the future of my kind? Assuming a way around the incompatibility with technology can be found. Representative stands up to reunite with the others. "Thank you for this conversation. I'll leave you to your work now." She turns and leaves through the open door.

"Well, Henrik, it's been fun talking to you, but now I think I should confer with my other selves." I leave through the open door. As I go down the corridor another parahuman rounds the corner in front of me. To my surprise he appears at first to be another of me. But, as I look closer and smell his scent, it becomes obvious that he is not only male but also has some rodent genes of some sort, as clear from his long tail with a small tuft at the end and his long whiskers and incisors. He seems just as surprised as me and bounds back down where he came from, muttering something that doesn't sound like Landlish or Lojban. My link to the ship's crew directory identifies him as Adham Ricardo, ship's purser, what was he doing down here I wonder?

"No, I don't think I'll bother you further, Morris." He looks slightly offended as I walk out the door to the Surgery. Did I say something wrong? A quick consultation with Representative suggests his ego was wounded slightly by my referral to him by name instead of title.

Strange how much importance they place on ego.

Decisions

The three of me reconvene, when in close proximity their memories synchronize more easily. I have access to the memories of all three interviews without the slightest time delay. I review them, all three brains working together to process the data. Within five minutes I am ready to start building consensus on the issues at hand.

First priority is the issue of microbots. Do I allow myself to be packed up in stasis for years if not decades, or become immortal? Even temporarily? The voyage will take a long time, yes, and there will be few experiences worth remembering on a small vessel such as this. But

Engineer assures that the drive I brought along can store centuries worth of memories, and if it gets even close to filled I can delete extraneous memories. Medic would like to examine the microbots, and would not have a chance to study them while in stasis. Representative does not feel strongly either way. Consensus is formed, we will take immortality, for now.

Second priority is whether to attempt to save any data on how to replicate presently discovered Federation technology. It is known that the Federal Guard typically reacts to any sign of nanotechnology on a quarantined world with orbital bombardment. However the antimatter production technology that Henrik alluded to may prove useful and is not specifically prohibited to my knowledge. Magnetic monopoles would be prohibited but there is no means of producing them on board in any case. Engineer believes that up to 50% of local memory storage should be devoted to downloading technical data. Medic thinks that more space should be left free for personal memories, maybe 25%. Representative agrees with Medic. Consensus formed, 30% of my local memory storage is dedicated specifically to technical data storage.

Third priority is which crewmembers to interview next. Online crew profiles indicate that there are four remaining crew and three bodies. I can interview three crew now and the remaining one later. But which ones? The remaining crew are Captain Shigeto Terryn, First Mate Gudrun Korba, Navigator Rika Fischer, and Purser Adham Ricardo. Captain Shigeto Terryn and First Mate Gudrun Korba were met previously at docking, and a quick comparison of his profile image to my memory indicates that Purser Adham Ricardo was the crewman Engineer briefly encountered as she was returning from the interview with Henrik. Of the four only Navigator Rika Fischer, an uplifted sea lion rather than a true parahuman, is the only member of the crew that none of my bodies have encountered in person. Engineer would like to speak with Purser Adham Ricardo, his morphology intrigues her somehow. Medic noticed some anatomical oddities in First Mate Gudrun Korba and would like a chance to examine her more closely. Representative feels that it might be useful to communicate with this "Captain", by my understanding the role of Captain is to act as some form of central coordinator for the rest of the crew. Why do they need to give their ideas and needs to a central source? Are they incapable of forming a consensus on their own without someone to coordinate them? I do not understand the function and must examine further. The three suggestions noted, consensus is formed and the three who shall be interviewed next are Purser Adham Ricardo, First Mate Gudrun Korba, and Captain Shigeto Terryn. Navigator Rika Fischer shall be contacted later.

Representative contacts Vicki again, asking the Artificial Intelligence to find the crew set to be interviewed and inform them of our desire to meet. "The Captain and the First Mate are in a private meeting." The pseudo-insectoid avatar informs me with a twinge of simulated regret. "Standing orders are to not allow any disturbances to either individual during such times. Previous data estimates that they will become available in approximately 50-70 minutes." Almost as an afterthought it adds, "Adham is currently in Engineering, but he has not indicated unavailability, shall I contact him now?"

Consensus needs to be revised. Two of the subjects are unavailable, two bodies will not be needed for some time. Representative suggests that one of us interview Navigator Rika Fischer while another interviews Adham. Engineer wants to interview Adham, Medic and Representative believe her expertise may be more useful speaking to Navigator Rika Fischer. Engineer acquiesces.

I ask Vicki where one could find Navigator Rika Fischer, it says that Rika is on the bridge, on duty but not too busy to talk. I send messages informing Adham and Rika of my desire to speak with them and they reply shortly after. Representative goes to speak with Adham, Engineer goes to speak with Rika, Medic reports to Dr. Morris' lab for medical examination prior to microbot injection.

Engineer feels an emotion I have no prior experience with, some kind of hostility towards Representative when the assignments are given out? Will need further investigation.

Meeting the Crew Reprise

Representative finds Adham Ricardo in engineering, at the time he is talking to Henrik. The intriguing blend of fox and rodent turns from his conversation as I enter to give me a bewildered look. "You're one of our passengers then?"

Medic returns to Dr. Taouchev's surgery. The grouchy tigeroo looks at me disdainfully. "Well?" He asks, with a bit of impatience. "Have you all decided yet?"

Engineer heads over to the bridge, the section is in free-fall and I feel momentarily disoriented before that body's inner ear sensations are cut off from the rest of the collective. The navigator, an Uplift rather than a Parahuman, spins in the air to face me as I enter the room. "Not used to microgravity yet?" Rika Fischer asks me.

I give the ship's purser a more in-depth look as I consider him. Large ears and pointed muzzle like mine, tan fur like mine, tail, thin and tipped with a tuft of brown fur instead of fluffy and black-tipped like mine. "I am your passenger, yes. I saw you earlier and wanted to discuss some things with you."

I give Dr. Taouchev my answer. "Yes. I have decided. All three of my bodies will be immortal for this journey. I will need all of their perspectives."

I struggle to get my response to the navigator out without the nausea that I've localized to the Engineer body overwhelming my vocal chords. "No, I haven't."

Henrik interrupts. "Wait," he interjects, "you're not the same one who spoke to me a few hours ago. Your mesh ID is different." Both the fox/otter and the fox/gerbil look puzzled. Adham asks, "I thought the one who met with Henrik was the one I spotted earlier?"

"Fine then." The tiger hybrid retorts. "First we will need a full body scan." He gestures to the body-sized cylinder laying open on the side in the center of the room. "I know that you have your own internal monitors, but you can understand that I would prefer to rely upon my own equipment, yes?"

The sea lion chuckles and giggles, "don't worry about it." She assures me. "You'll get used to it soon enough." She pivots and slowly glides towards me. "So, what was it you wanted to talk about?"

"I am the Emilia Collective." I inform Adham and Henrik. "I used a different node to converse with Henrik earlier than I am using to converse with the two of you now but I am the same person. I remember our conversation," I state gesturing to the otter hybrid, "and I remember you turning back when I spotted you," I tell the rodent hybrid.

I start to grow slightly suspicious at the suggestion. Could Taouchev want to analyze the implants that enable me to exist across so many bodies for the Federation's own purposes? No, I dismiss the idea as nonsense. The Federation would have already seized the schematics as soon as they had exiled my parents and killed the radical faction. The only major improvements that had been made in the past few centuries were in the materials. And those refinements were only needed because I didn't have nanotechnology to fabricate my implants like the Federation did. Nanotechnology like I was going to infuse my bodies with. Seeing no point in resisting, I lay Medic down on the scanning bed.

As the motion sickness starts to pass I tell her my reason for being in this null-gravity hellhole. "I wanted to know about your function on this ship, how you guide it across the lightyears between stars?"

"Right," Adham says, exasperated, "I remember hearing about that before we launched. "So why are you using a different one now?"

The multi-function body scanner takes the better part of an hour to complete the assorted ultrasonic, thermographic, magnetic, and other various types of medical analysis it can perform. Once it has finished Dr. Taouchev tells me to lie down on a different bed, next to a device that has a pair of clear plastic tubes tipped with syringe heads that seem to be almost a full centimeter wide at the tips.

Rika outright laughs at me. "The navigation is mostly done by computers. Pretty much all I do is check their math and react in unexpected situations. Even computers don't know how to handle everything. You met the AI yet?"

"That node was specialized for technical analysis and processing." I tell Adham. "This node is trained in social interaction and advocating. It was determined that this node would be better suited for this interview with you." I feel a momentary twinge of that strange emotion across the mesh again. "In any case, I wished to hear about your particular purpose on this ship. As far as I can tell it is something to do with resource allocation, yes?"

The tiger hybrid picks up one of the heads of the IV feeds, which begins to fill with a clear fluid with barely visible metallic flecks, and begins to draw it towards my side. "I attempt to limit the pain from this kind of thing." He informs me, not too reassuringly, "but there will be some pain." He sticks the needle directly into my femoral vein. There is a brief moment of sharp pain that ceases as abruptly as it began, replaced by a feeling of pressure in my thigh as the fluid is pumped in. "Every few months you'll have to come in here to have the damaged microbots removed," he picks up the other feed, "this one will circulate your blood out and filter it, while the other returns it with fresh microbots. It'll take two or three hours to run, though this session will only take one hour. Will that be a problem?"

I recollect the odd virtual entity that assured me it wasn't self-aware. "Yes, I have. So are you just a safeguard then? Someone who heads off problems before they get out of hand?"

The fennec/gerbil grins and glances at me over the tip of his muzzle. "A bit like that." He admits, "it's rather more complicated than that. Do you use money in your economy?" I know about the concept, historically, a means of decentralizing distribution of resources, inefficient. I quickly tell him "no" and he continues. "Well, most planets do have some form of currency, whether they call them credits or thalers or augrams or qcoins, and a major part of my job is determining the exchange rates between the various currencies used by the different planets that we visit. Most of the Federation uses production credits redeemable for raw materials and fabrication time on the public nanofabricators, the exact value varies from system to system outside the stargate network but within the network the Centauri production credit is the standard unit of value. It's what I usually use as a standard when exchanging currencies too." He continues on his lecture. "It gets more complicated with centrally planned economies, there we have to deal with entire governments instead of individual sellers, and that usually ends up large scale barter. Or the gift economies. "Give me that thing or do this thing for me and I'll leave a good review for you, so maybe later someone will be inclined to do something for you." It's so ridiculous, we usually end up introducing a currency to them just to make things easier."

I tell him "no," I can probably have my bodies take turns with the procedure and task the other two for whatever is needed. The group was designed with a degree of redundancy. It occurs to me that the procedure should be done for Medic in time to meet with the two ranking officers on the ship. In the meantime, I open Medic's senses to a full real-time stream from Engineer and Representative, tuning out her local perceptions almost in the entirety.

The pinniped bobs her head up and down. I think that's an "affirmative". "Pretty much," she admits. "Did you want to see the interface now?" She swerves again, at this distance I can detect magnetic fields emanating from just below her skin to grasp the metallic walls. As I watch she drifts over to a bed with multiple restraining devices and electrodes affixed to the top.

What Adham is talking about is bizarre, I can't understand this need to "exchange" one thing for another that he's referring to. I tell him that it makes no sense, why not simply transfer resources to where they're needed most? "Well," he continues, "that's what traders do. We bring goods and services from someplace where they're abundant to a place where they're scarce, and then take whatever's abundant there to someplace else. Keeping some for ourselves to keep us running of course, but not as much as a central planning bureaucracy would take. It's more efficient to go from the bottom-up so to speak."

I look on, intrigued, as Rika floats over to the bed. As she approaches the leads trailing from the shelf snake out towards her and plug themselves in with robotic precision. Some manner of motors in the cables themselves? They would have to be microscopic, possibly nanotechnology. It's unsettling how much they take nanotech for granted. My interface chimes with an invitation to stream her viewpoint as she plugs in and more motile cables secure her to the platform, I accept.

Ah, I see now, with multiple individuals you need someone to coordinate them. "My precursors agreed. My nodes have no central planning, my decisions are made as a consensus by all the component parts. When resources are needed the nodes on site communicate directly with the nodes that have the resources and the means to transport them. It is simple and efficient."

My interface is overwhelmed with data from the stream, icons for literally everything on the ship it seems. Navigational headings, fuel supplies, matter stockpiles, structural integrity, I forward most of the data to Medic so that Engineer can function in this new environment but still more than half of what remains has to be canceled or blocked before I dare trying to move that body. I stare at the one, single sea lion hovering over the console, "so much data," I say, exasperated, "how do you keep track of it all?"

Adham looks skeptical, "and no one along this supply chain tries to take more than is needed? No one thinks that they deserve more than others for any reason?"

Rika shakes a couple of the connectors out and turns back to face me. "I have an array of agent programs set on this console and in my implants to handle most mundane tasks. Generally only the most important or urgent things are brought to my attention. And in any case when we're performing complex maneuvers like docking or combat my senses are locked out, the others would need to disconnect me manually to even try communicating with me in those cases." So, I notice, she has to use external mind-simulations to handle this workload and still has to shut down external communication to make full use. How many bodies would a collective such as myself need to fly this ship?

Engineer suddenly redirects her attention from her surroundings to the feed from Representative and her conversation with Adham Ricardo. She picks up the emotional charge from Representative and reacts for reasons largely unknown to her.

I get confused again. "Why would such a thing be tolerated? Devoting disproportionate resources to one node benefits the one division at the expense of the whole." I get a twinge of regret over the mesh, why?

"Well," Adham says, "we have to tolerate it because everybody thinks that they deserve more resources than everybody else. They all want to consume, breed, and conquer more than anyone else."

I refuse to believe that. "That's not true. I..." I pause, in my case there is only one me, every one of my bodies is simply a division of me. One body hoarding resources hurts me as a whole but these others are not me. What could my attitude towards their resources be?

As I think Adham's eyes lose focus for a few minutes as he reviews something through his implants. Finally finished with whatever he was doing he looks back at me now. "The mesh data says that your, "precursors" did you call them? It says that half of them attempted to kill off every other hive mind so that they could attempt to take over the universe themselves. It also says there were three group intellects that survived and were exiled to your world. What happened to the other two?"

I feel rage, anger. "All three died!" I shout at them. "They made me and then terminated themselves for being obsolete. Their plan was to distill the galaxy's population into a single genotype that could form a single unified collective. And then all the imperfect other collectives would die off so their child could take over. So they made me from all their genes, taught me everything they knew, and died. Leaving me all alone." I trail off on that last syllable, my voice tinged with emotions I had not experienced since long before this body was ever decanted.

"Oh," Adham says, apologetic. "I'm sorry, I didn't realize..." I don't heard what he says next as I storm out of the room and head back to my cabin to meet up with the rest of me.

"You okay?" Engineer brings her focus back to her immediate surroundings. Rika is hovering near me, looking concerned. I'd allowed two of my bodies to lose their awareness of their surroundings, and I had canceled the stream from the ship's systems. What was happening to me?

All three of my selves retreat into my cabin after that confrontation with Ricardo. The difference between our two civilizations seems insurmountable, how could a group mind and a society of singletons coexist when singletons not only accepted, but required such an inefficient distribution of resources? It was obscene, ludicrous. I can understand why my forebears had wanted to attempt merging into single collective consciousnesses and how frustrating their failure must have been.

    I am still occupied with that line of thought when Vicki informs me that Captain Shigeto Terryn and First Mate Gudrun Korba are ready to see me now. Medic is reminded of her prior interest in Gudrun's unusual anatomy. Representative wants to compare her role to the Captain's. Engineer, who was most upset by what Purser Ricardo said, is advised to receive microbots now.

    My nodes query their destinations and depart. I note that Medic and Representative appear to be traveling to the same area, while Engineer simply needs to draw upon my memory to find the medical bay.

    Engineer arrives at the facility maintained by the tiger-kangaroo and simply informs him that she is here to receive the microbot implants. He shows her to the chair with the blood filters and she sits down, anticipating the probes before they insert themselves.

    Medic and Representative are led by the ship's internal maps to the same cabin, where both the Captain and First Mate apparently reside. The canine and the feline stand outside the door to welcome my nodes. They are dressed in the same outfits that they wore when greeting me at the docking bay, but Korba appears to have green stripes now for some reason. "You wished to speak with the two of us?" Captain Terryn asks. Representative affirms. He waves us into the room. This cabin is even larger than the one occupied by my three nodes, I notice a track along the ceiling running perpendicular to the walls dividing the room in half. When Engineer remotely processes that data she supposes that it supports a retractable wall between two normal-sized cabins.

Representative turns to the Captain in query. "The two of you merged your cabins?"

Medic addresses the First Mate with her first question. "How did your fur pattern change in the time since we met last?"

Captain Shigeto Terryn looks slightly uneasy at my question. "Myself and First Mate Korba have a recurring relationship and we're currently in one of our intimate phases. During such a phase we tend to sleep together most nights and it's most efficient to merge cabins, when we decide to take a break the partition is raised easily enough." He waves a hand idly towards a wall opposite the track. "Envoy Fairhold prefers to have time alone so zie tends to have the partition to zir cabin raised. If zie decides to join us the partition is lowered for the night."

First Mate Gudrun Korba on the other hand seems excited. "I'm a Kitsune." She replies, pointing to her collection of tails. As I watch the fur around her face begins to change color to a deep blue, the hair on her cranium lengthens at the pace of a millimeter every five minutes while her cheek ruffs become thinner, and her fingers sprout claws.

While these conversations are occurring, Engineer hears a familiar-sounding voice with her node's own ears talking to the Surgeon. Eventually Dr. Morris pokes his head in and asks me a question. "It seems you have a visitor. Shall I let him in?"

Representative considers the situation. "This alters the plan slightly. If both of you wish to be interviewed simultaneously there is a reduced need for two nodes to converse with you. This node has not yet obtained the microbots the surgeon claims are needed to survive interstellar travel and could be acquiring them at the same time as the Engineer node."

Medic is confused. "What is a Kitsune and why would that allow you to alter your physiology so readily?"

Engineer wonders who could be coming to visit her. Her curiosity piqued she tells Morris to "let him in."

Terryn glances over at Medic for a second then turns back to Representative. "It would seem that your other 'node' is keeping my first mate occupied. If you had questions for me alone you could ask them while Gudrun is being interrogated about her little quirks."

"Oh, yes." Gudrun Korba concedes. "You have been isolated, you may not know who we are. We are a subculture who employ internal bodysculpting microbots to alter and enhance our bodies. The microbots controlled by our BCI implants can shift cells around and modify their functions in accordance with our thoughts." She picks up a couple of her tails to show me. "These are both an indication of my rank within the order and a reservoir of spare mass. A trainee with only one tail can change their coloration. A two-tailed initiate can alter their build enough to resemble any other member of their species and sex. Three tails and one can change their apparent sex and assume the physiology of a range of species." Korba releases her tails and lets all of them fan out. "I'm afraid I'm sworn to secrecy in regards to what one of my rank is capable of."

Adham Ricardo enters the medical bay. His ears lowered as he looks at Engineer lying on the chair. "Excuse me." He says, his voice soft. "I was wondering if you would accept an apology from me in regards to what I said to your other... self?"

"Very well." Representative says. "I am intrigued by your apparent function on board this craft. If I manage to devise what it entails this node may leave discussion of your 'relationships' to Medic when she finishes discussing Kitsune with Korba."

"I am having trouble discerning the function of you 'Kitsune', First Mate Korba." Medic inquires. "It seems that it would be more efficient to adapt permanent specialists for different tasks than to modify an individual to change functions on the fly."

Engineer lets out a soft exhalation, I don't know exactly what that meant but somehow I knew it indicated slight annoyance or exasperation.

"We are all one person. What you say to me will be heard by all three of us on this craft."

Shigeto waves a hand and segments of the floor rose up to form four chairs, in two pairs facing each other. He takes a seat in one of the chairs and points at the one facing his. After a minute he says "I suggest you sit down here and our pairs take the other seats." At this prompting Representative does so. "You say that you cannot ascertain what I do for the ship? I am the Captain, I coordinate the other crewmembers and make decisions that affect the entire ship, that makes me responsible for their actions."

Korba sits and waits for Medic to sit opposite her before she begins to explain. "There are many who believe that an individual should acquire as many different skillsets as possible so as to be prepared for any situation, and that methodology is very useful when you're in a situation with few people available. But that's not why Kitsune shapeshift." She lays her tails over her lap and begins to stroke them idly. "No, we change forms in order to disrupt society."

Ricardo leans against a nearby table and begins to speak. "I just wanted to say I was sorry for that outburst before. I hadn't realized it would upset, you, so badly. I suppose I had just forgotten how hard it can be to try and understand a new system like that." He cocks an ear at me quizzically. "Are you alright? Something I said?"

Representative is intrigued for a minute. "You make decisions for the entire ship? I would have thought it inefficient to route all decisions through a single node instead of allowing the nodes immediately relevant to the issue to decide based on the needs of the whole. Especially without our memory-sharing technology."

Medic tries to contain her utter confusion at Korba's statement. "Why? Why would such actions be allowed by the whole?"

Engineer answers "if you are referring to my apparent distraction my Representative and Medic nodes are having rather confusing conversations with Captain Shigeto Terryn and First Mate Gudrun Korba. You may continue." When he doesn't immediately resume I ask him "you mentioned something about forgetting how hard it is to try and understand a new system, elaborate."

"Well, no." Shigeto accedes. "I don't need to make every decision for the crew, if one of them can solve a problem on their own I don't get involved. It's only if they need to draw from the ship's resources that I need to interfere with their work. If there's a dispute between two or more crewmembers I cast the tie-breaking vote. I also propose a course for the ship to follow when we are starting on a new commercial enterprise or looking for work."

Korba gives a soft chuckle. "Oh, the whole of society doesn't quite tolerate our actions, there are plenty of objectors. But for the most part people find our antics to be amusing, at worst an annoyance."

Adham sighs, his ears drooping visibly. "I was not born to the Federation, I come from one of the "Outworlds", as much a part of the Federation as your own world, but radically different it would seem."

Representative thinks she's beginning to understand. "I suppose that arrangement makes sense with your less efficient methods of communication. But could you explain why you specifically have this role?"

Medic seems to be getting a little frustrated. "You've explained how people react to your "Kitsune" group's actions but you still haven't explained what it is you do or why?"

Engineer stares at Adham, intrigued. "My memory banks lack information on your world, would you care to explain what makes it so different?"

Captain Terryn pauses before answering, as if he has to think hard to come up with an explanation. "Well, for one thing I own the ship. I took out several loans to buy the design plans, constructor microbots, mineral rights, and assorted other little things needed to build this spacecraft and I spent almost my entire share of three voyages' profits on paying back those loans."

Gudrun Korba shrugs at me. "Yes, I suppose I haven't told you yet. In Federation space we strive to prevent stagnation. Stagnation leads to apathy, apathy leads to tyranny, and tyranny kills civilizations. We have two primary methods to head off stagnation: the first and most common is to disrupt the status quo in a variety of methods that don't cause lasting harm but still change the state of things. One time we made all the food from the public nanofabs in SecLand's East sector taste like sewage for instance."

Ricardo grimaces as he remembers what life was once like for him. "On my old homeworld, ownership of arable land was concentrated in the hands of a small number of hereditary landlords. After the forced settlement technology regressed to pre-industrial levels, by the time I left there were barely any forms of automation available, as such there existed a caste of people who were considered to be little more than living tools, slaves."

Representative continues her line of inquiry towards the captain. "And, this ownership gives you control over the ship in what way? Why did the crew agree to follow you?"

Medic searches the mesh for the definition of "tyranny", the search provides "rule by an absolute ruler, often oppressive. See: Tyrant." The proceeding definition of "tyrant" indicates "an absolute ruler, usually oppressive and cruel." She asks Korba to elaborate on how tyranny "kills civilizations."

Engineer is surprised. People used as tools? Their labors benefiting another without any gain for themselves? Even used in place of robots? She notes the tone Adham used when speaking the term used for such people and asks "what was your social status on that world?"

"Well, basically, the government's law enforcement recognizes me as the ship's owner and anyone else who tried to command the ship would be investigated." Shigeto explains. "And it's not like the crew have no say in ship decisions, they can voice their opinions at any time, or just leave the next time we come into port."

Korba starts to give a more detailed explanation. "Tyrants suppress anything that could present a threat to their rule. In particular change, change upsets the established order even when it improves the living conditions of the general populace. Not to mention that concentration of power in a single individual and his cronies makes the collapse all the more devastating when it happens."

Adham groans as he thinks about it. "I will admit it, I was taken as a slave when I was about nine standard years old. The slavers thought I might make a good pleasure slave so they removed my gonads, and in any case hybrids like myself weren't well regarded on that world. But a few years after I was sold my master noticed I was good with numbers and had me educated as an accountant." I notice that his hands are trembling as he recounts this story. "Yet, he, his sons, and even his wives and daughters would still force me into bed with them frequently."

Representative considers this concept of "ownership". "So, you possess this ship because the rules of your state that you do on account of what you've done? Is that how it works?"

"But wouldn't preventing drastic change prevent the civilization from falling?" Medic attempted to rebut Korba's argument. "Especially if the tyrant is immortal like your technology is capable of accomplishing?"

Engineer tries to parse this information, it all seems so bizarre. "What, pleasures are you talking about? I don't understand what could require removal of your reproductive organs?"

Shigeto pauses and considers. "Yes, I suppose that's correct. But I would like to mention that several societies have attempted to do away with the concept of ownership, and with the exception of yours, if you can call your hive mind a "society", they all collapse or revert to stone age barbarism within a generation."

Korba laughs again. "Nobody can live forever, even with our technology several Praetors have died in office from assassinations, accidents, or microbot glitches. The human country of Zhōngguó was unified as a strong centralized state by an Emperor who thought he could live forever but he perished a mere eleven years after his rise to power, and the country fell into civil war three years into his son's reign. Some dynasties that succeeded them held together for two centuries or more but they all inevitably fell to usurpers. Nippon, the country from whose mythology we take our name, decentralized power under a dynasty of Emperors believed to be descendants of the god of the sun and who presided over many reforms in government in an unbroken line that persisted for over 2,500 years."

"Right," Adham states. "You all have identical bodies, so that would mean you're all female, right?" At my affirmation he continues. "During puberty hormones produced by the male gonads trigger muscular growth and other secondary dimorphisms. A number of slave owning masters enjoyed copulating with pre-pubescents, by neutering me young it was ensured that I would never go through puberty and develop the muscles to fight off those who might force themselves into me." I noticed him idly rubbing at his crotch as he spoke, "I asked Morris to clone me a new pair of balls as soon as I escaped that world."

Representative starts to understand. "I see, so the government is necessary to prevent disputes over who has the right to use certain resources or assets? And you believe that I don't need a government because there are no disputes over ownership on my-" She stops, realizing what she was about to say.

Medic calls up some of my information on religions. "God of the sun you say?" She inquires. "Similar to the Last Solar Prophet?"

Engineer feels something odd at Adham's story, the only thing that comes close in my memory is her reaction to witnessing a node crushed in an industrial accident. The falling machine had slain her too quickly to broadcast any painful memories, but the sight of her spilled blood and smashed organs on the floor had left the surviving nodes on site, and many others within broadcast range before the stream had been temporarily cut off by safeguards, catatonic. Not understanding why she was feeling this again now she struggled to voice her next question. "How, how did you manage to escape from that awful place?"

Shigeto grins. "Yes, and you only own your planet because the

Federation recognizes your right to own it and the other polities cannot reach it."

Korba chortles, "I'm actually unsure of whether we came up with that idea. There's no records of the Kitsune Order's existence at the time Noospherism emerged, but it may have been some of our precursors. It is true that the dynasty of the House of Silver seems to provide the ideal balance between stability and dynamism."

Adham's facial features raise as he remembers this now. "I actually had help from this ship's crew. When they arrived in orbit the heads of the major families, my master included, were invited to a summit to discuss trade with the Defiance's crew. First Mate Korba noticed me being yanked around on a chain tied around my neck and began to talk to me while my master was distracted negotiating with the captain. She told me about life in the Federation, and after some cajoling I confessed my feelings towards my master to her." He looks at me thoughtfully. "She did a better job of hiding her disgust and horror than you are, but she's trained in that sort of thing. Anyways, on the last day of the summit she handed me a pill and a note reading that if I wanted to be free I should swallow the pill an hour before the next time my master became intimate with me. It turned out to be a tailored strain of the influenza virus, while me and the majority of others it infected became ill for a few days my master and his family, and many other landowners whom he was related to, drowned in their own bodily fluids."

Representative is slightly disturbed by this realization that my prolonged existence apart from the rest of parahumanity is only at the will of the only parahuman government capable of destroying me entirely.

Medic considers the merits of Korba's statement. "And I suppose that this dynasty enables you to remove potential tyrants without completely destroying Federation society. In contrast to Adham Ricardo's world."

Engineer is reminded of how the Federal Guard reacted to my precursors, and even though I know Adham's masters probably deserved it, this part of the story disturbs me. "I thought that the Federation did not interfere in Outworld governments, except to prevent them from acquiring nanotechnology?"

Korba stares at Medic, her eyes seem to bore into her like industrial drills. "That country on that planet was already primed to topple. We simply provided the tools for them to bring themselves down."

Adham snorts. "Oh, but this wasn't the Federation interfering in an Outworld government. It was just a Federation citizen gifting an Outworld native with a bit of biotechnology that would not present a threat to anyone with a microbot immune system. It did not matter what I chose to do with it. Of course," he notes, "after that power vacuum opened I couldn't go back to my old life. But fortunately, the Defiance sent down a shuttle to the region and sold the former slaves weapons to maintain their new independence and passage to their old homelands or even to the Federation. I chose to leave the planet behind entirely."

Representative and Medic disengage from their conversations and grasp hands. The optical sensors in their palms line up and exchange data at rapid speed, far more quickly and with greater fidelity than even direct user-to-user wi-fi can transmit. Thoughts that cannot be truly translated into words arc back and forth between the two as they contemplate the data presented to them.

Engineer picks up glimpses of the other nodes' thoughts as she thinks of what to say next to Ricardo. "What is the difference between the concept of ownership on your old world and in the Federation?" She eventually decides on.

Shigeto and Gudrun glance at one another and seem to exchange a series of subtle expressions, I am too preoccupied to parse them out. Eventually, the captain speaks to me, "would you like us to leave you be for a while now?"

Adham Ricardo stares at me, "I have studied the economic systems of dozens of worlds, all of them have the concept of property, whether it belongs to the individual, or the state, or the tribe. As a rule, denial of property rights to individuals inhibits technological or social progress.

What can be property also varies a great deal, but the pattern I've noticed is that when land can be owned it enables ownership of people, and landowning individualist societies may or may not practice slavery but landowning groups always have slaves."

"Yes, we would." Representative and Medic speak in unison as they get up to leave.

Engineer looks at Adham, pleading something, but what is unclear. "What do you consider my concept of property to be most like?"

"Goodbye, Emilia, we hope to speak to you again later."

"You're complicated," Adham replies. "You're both an individual and a culture all to yourself, and you don't seem to have even considered yourself to have "owned" anything as you have had so little contact with anyone else."

At this point Dr. Morris Taouchev comes back in and tells me that the procedure is complete. The leads in Engineer's body retract and she is free to leave, Representative and Medic call out to her to confer. "Thank you for this most enlightening conversation, Adham Ricardo, I have much to think about now." I leave.

History of The Kitsune

Kitne, Huli-jin, shifters, cubi, whatever they're called, this semi-secret society strikes fear in the hearts of overbearing Emissaries and cruel heads of house. Most of the public, however, see them as folk heroes of a sort, visiting punishment on those too well-connected for the legal system to touch. Given all they've done it's a wonder that the Kitsune order hasn't been rooted out and exiled yet.

The reasoning, like so many other things in the Federation, goes back to the Silver Houses. In the century following the Gene Wars, when the silver fox phenotype was re-emerging from the survivors of genus Argentum, one young vixen discovered that her parents had secretly altered her genes in-vitro to turn her fur black and white. The exact details of the genetic fraud vary from telling to telling, as the case files were sealed after dismissal from lack of evidence, even the vixen's true name is unknown. What the stories do agree on is that her disgust with her family led her to assume a new name dredged up from the archives on Terran mythology, Kumiho.

As the years went on, Kumiho was attributed to the public relations downfalls of dozens, if not hundreds of corrupt politicians. She learned their dirty secrets through hacking, networking, and outright seduction, wearing a different face each time. Civil forces raided bodysculpting boutiques to find her, but none of them had any record of servicing any parahumans with the looks she'd been recorded with. The obvious conclusion was that she had assistants, the secrets posted by "Kumiho" must have been actually from a number of different people. But even then facial recognition drew a blank.

It wasn't until two hundred years later that one of her followers revealed the truth. On a live stream from a dozen different cameras a doe transformed into a male weasel with four tails in a matter of minutes. As their fur changed color and their flesh and bones warped and popped they explained to the astonished press that they were a member of a secret society of cyborgs founded by Kumiho.

Their body had been laced with motile micromachinery that could reconfigure to alter their appearance with a signal from their BCI. When they had first joined the society their natural skin was replaced with an artificial substitute that could extend or withdraw fur with variable pigmentation at will. As they accomplished assignments their connective tissues were replaced with micromachines that could detach or attach on command and extra tails were granted to them to show their progression up the society's hierarchy and store spare protoplasm. Kumiho, according to them, had ten tails and had progressed to the point where, it was rumored, her neurons had been replaced by microbots.

For reasons unclear, the civil guard were ordered not to move until this explanation was complete. At that point the speaker made their escape, disappearing into the crowd effortlessly. Shortly after, a group of senators introduced legislation specifically licensing the existence of the society, which they named the "Kitsune" order on the advice of Terran scholars, so long as they refrained from committing capital crimes and policed their own, which they seem to have agreed to. The few times a Kitsune was indicated to be involved in a murder or act of terror a shredded body stripped of all micromachinery was discovered in a ditch shortly after. There are even a few cases where mercantile houses have specifically sought out Kitsune as representatives, though there is the possibility that they're merely copycats using knock-offs of the Kitsune cybernetics.

Sharing the Wealth: The Federation Economy in Detail

Due to the prevalence of automation and nanotechnology there are very few jobs in Federation space in the fields of mining, agriculture, or manufacturing, and the ones that exist are primarily supervision and programming of robots. Almost all manual labor is performed by machines, and with nanotechnology one can have a factory and recycling complex on their desk.

When automation all but eliminated manual labor in the Republic of New Pallas the government was faced with the prospect of hundreds of thousands of unemployed citizens, the obvious solution was to instate a guaranteed basic income that was enough to keep everyone fed and healthy, half the population was still living in state-owned arcology apartments anyway. For a couple centuries population expansion was carefully regulated to keep pace with the resources available and the progress of the terraforming operation and most seemed happy. Some of the permanently unemployed spent their time just soaking up entertainment, yes, but many others became artists, amateur scientists, or full-time parents.

Then there was the Plague War. The Republic was not hurt as badly as the SPPS but death spread throughout the arcologies regardless. While automated infrastructure remained intact its minders did not, breakdowns became increasingly commonplace leading to starvation. In addition, many parahumans became wary of packing so many people together in the immense but still confined city-buildings and fled to the largely unused countryside in droves. Desktop nanofabbers had become a luxury consumer product in the years before the plague, and some groups had (illegally) hacked them to self-replicate, now the starving masses were shoveling random plants and raw dirt into bootleg fabbers simply to eat.

Some in government tried to brand them as criminals, but they didn't have the resources left to enforce those laws and the politicians in question didn't last the next election cycle. Once able to operate in the open nanofab homesteads cropped up all over the continent, many of them nearly self-sufficient. But nanotechnology cannot turn lead into gold, raw elements still needed to be found and mined, often only after a significant investment of time and resources.

Joint-stock companies or corporations were never accepted as a legal entity in New Pallas, the corporations who created and enslaved their ancestors were too thoroughly demonized in their culture. Rather most businesses operate as independent contractors or at most partnerships with employees. However, a system of profit-sharing and crowdfunding has emerged that fulfills most of the functions of a corporation.

Profit-sharing is a system in which an individual citizen sets up a program to automatically distribute the profits from their work, after expenses of course, to specific people. Usually those people are friends or close relatives, but if some of them were people who gave them a significant amount of money when they were just starting their business then so be it. Each of New Pallas' founding genera has a profit-share in which each member contributes a small portion of their income, generally a small fraction of a percentage given the populations of every founding genus, which is distributed equally to every member of the genus. Smaller families also tend to have their own profit-shares, most notably Psi-Comm for the high families of genus Argentum.

Crowdfunding can generally be sorted into three categories: pre-orders, subscriptions, or loans. Pre-orders are for specific projects with a discrete start and end, backers receive a reward at the completion of the project that they specified at funding (like Kickstarter). Subscriptions give the backers exclusive access, or at least early access, to the creator's content (i.e. Patreon). Loans are just what they sound like, backers expect to be paid back with interest at some point.

In practice, most citizens have a steady income from a combination of profit-shares and crowdfunding. The net result is that everyone eats, anyone can afford luxuries with some degree of saving, and artisans, inventors, and primary producers are the most affluent members of society. Interstellar merchants are a bit of an exception to this rule, but they're an extremely small minority.

Spacer Survival Gear:

The ForgePlate: A flat device usually 30 cm long by 6 wide and 3 cm thick. It's essentially a portable nanofabber, the user pours raw materials on the "feed" side and the internal mechanisms disassemble it to reassemble into the requested item, which is extruded through the "fab" side. To idiot-proof there's arrows indicating the direction material is supposed to go. Both working sides of the ForgePlate are covered with a nanomotile membrane that selectively lets materials through while maintaining a vacuum state within the device. The ForgePlate is operated by an external device, usually the user's BCI or a tablet computer, and comes pre-loaded with several designs though it can produce anything that a normal nanofab can so long as two of its dimensions fit within the length and width of the fabbing side, it can even self-replicate or produce a scaled-up version of itself. Given time and materials a single ForgePlate could potentially rebuild an entire civilization, for that reason spacers traveling to Outworlds are advised to integrate self-destruct mechanisms into their ForgePlates that activate when an unauthorized user attempts access.

Frontiersbeing Blaster: One of the most common plasma arc weapons on the market, the Frontiersbeing blaster remains popular for its reliability and versatility. The size of a large handgun, with a capacitor under the laser and quadruple ionization prongs. The laser ionizes air in a straight path from the prongs to the target, turning it into a conductive plasma capable of carrying a charge. The intensity of the laser and charge are determined by a slider on the side of the capacitor, at the "practice" setting the prongs aren't active and the laser is little more than a pointer to mark targets, while at its lower "powered" settings (usually marked in green) the beam carries a charge similar to that of a 20th century taser, this range of settings is colloquially known as "stun" and usually leaves no lasting damage worse than a first- or second degree burn. In the yellow-marked middle-range or "kill" settings it leaves a third-degree burn at the point of contact and carries a charge strong enough to kill most parahumans, though they can usually be revivified with quick application of microbots (although their internal bots might be shorted out). The settings marked in red, however, produce a plasma bolt hot enough to flash-boil subcutaneous tissue in a small area, producing a small and messy explosion. While these highest power levels might be considered overkill on an unarmored parahuman target it is quite useful when hunting larger fauna that can weather the shock from a yellow setting and it can even punch a hole in light Non-Newtonian armor, and while not advertised a headshot at full power can reliably prevent revivification. It's completely useless against non-conductive solid armor like kevlar of course. The standard capacitor holds enough power for 30 seconds of prolonged fire on the lowest green setting, 15 seconds on yellow, or 3 at max power; the original battery can fully charge the capacitor five times before needing a recharge itself, but that requires several minutes of downtime.

A World Lost:

Ferrikesh splayed his pedipalps across the copper wires and brackets splayed out before him on the workbench. His three arms worked fastidiously to give form to his latest idea, a longer-wave generator. His earlier wave sensor had picked up short waves of a millimeter or less emanating from the Visitors, those odd bilaterally symmetrical beings that had descended from the stars seven years ago and begun to teach some of their far superior science to the lowly kershkans, but this one should be able to generate waves of a decimeter or more in length. He was certain that the waves were some manner of communication between Visitors that no kershkan would be able to perceive, without his inventions, and he knew that the longer waves were used the further he was from a Visitor. However, he'd never seen them generate waves of more than a millimeter in length, with this he could surpass them for sure. That would show those oh-so-superior suited beings with their odd double-limbs.

Ferrikesh connected the last couple of wires, double-checked that everything was in place, then connected the final lead to the acid generator he used to power his inventions. There was a brief spark as he connected that lead and a faint hum but nothing else immediately obvious. He picked up his sensor and checked the paper scroll feeding out as the tiny needle marked it. Success! It was close to 1.4 decimeters long.

Immediately the kershkan inventor thought of applications, he could use pulses of these waves to send some sort of signal from one side of town to the other, it would revolutionize communication. And without those messy long wires the Visitors had been setting up lately for them. Sure, he might not be able to cast voices or images through these waves like they could with the wires, yet, but they could be set up anywhere, without the Visitors' infrastructure. Ferrikesh was suddenly reminded by a loss of feeling in one leg that he hadn't eaten in a couple of days, he decided that he had better celebrate with a couple of drak-beast pies down at the marketplace and left the house. He was so intent on his goal that he didn't even notice the flying machines swooping in on his home from all directions as he ran to catch a steam cart.

Ferrikesh came back, two of his hands still dripping with grease, to find his house surrounded by Visitors. Their spindly machines loped or flew around the perimeter and pulled knick-knacks and furniture from the house while suited figures examined the assorted debris. There were variations of course but in general the Visitors were covered from their protruding heads to their two feet and lifted stabilizing appendages in what appeared to be heavy cloth of differing colors. What he presumed were respiratory spiracles at the front of the head were covered in a bizarre apparatus of pipes and vents, their lightspots by a pair of dark glass lenses. The Visitors had claimed that they came from worlds that received less sunlight and were colder with a much lower oxygen content to the air, hence the suits for their comfort, but Ferrikesh had suspicions that they simply didn't want to expose their potential weaknesses to the barbaric natives.

Outraged by this indignity Ferrikesh dashed towards the interlopers, two of his three legs forward and pumping hard. As he came near one of the Visitors looked up and two of the flying machines turned to level guns at him. Ferrikesh stopped, he knew from demonstrations that unlike kershkan firearms the Visitors' guns could be loaded with multiple bullets which they could fire in sequence and rapidly. He stopped, rotating his head to bring his light spots to bear on the suited figures and deadly machines in turn.

Eventually, one Visitor wearing a suit colored in patches of white and black, their leader, Selene of Clan Argentum if he remembered right, approached him. She was carrying a mass of tangled wires and brass that with some trepidation Ferrikesh recognized as his wave generator. The Visitor made a quick warbling sound followed by a flat mechanical voice speaking in Ferrikesh's native language. "Did you make this?" It asked.

His pride and indignation temporarily overwhelming his sense of self-preservation Ferrikesh replied "yes, I did. What of it?"

As soon as he said that Selene tossed the invention on the ground, lifted one long foot, and stomped down on it. She brought her foot down on it again and again until nothing but smashed wires and shattered woodwork remained. "If you value your world, you will not try that again." The Visitor leader's device translated her language as.

"Why?!" Ferrikesh shouted. "Why did you do that? How did you even know it was there?"

"We detected it." Was his only response as the Visitors moved to their vehicle, parked on the other side of the debris pile.

"You can detect those waves?" The kershkan said incredulously. "But, you never used them. I never picked them up around you." He babbled.

One of the larger Visitors, dressed in dark blue and carrying a rifle stopped and addressed him. "What do you mean you never picked them up?"

Ferrikesh bent down and rooted through the pile until he found his wave sensor. "This responds in your presence." He told them, switching it on and watching the paper spool out with many waves drawn on the slip. "I thought maybe you didn't know about the longer waves, that was why I never found any around you. I guess you have some other sinister reason for not generating waves that long." He accused.

The blue-coated Visitor and Selene directed their faces at each other, Ferrikesh noted a spike in activity on his sensor, and then Selene turned back to him. "If you want to know. If you really want to know, come with us." She gestured at the vehicle, turbines starting to wind up.

Ferrikesh looked nervously at the Visitor vehicle, he knew that some kershkans had been allowed in to the Visitors' outpost, even been allowed to see what was under their suits some said, but they were sworn to secrecy about most of what had gone on inside. He admitted to being a tad anxious about what could happen there, but at the same time he knew he wouldn't get a better chance to learn about the mysterious Visitors. He stepped towards them, one foot forward.

The kershkan inventor spent the next two hours trying to make himself comfortable in a vehicle without seats designed for his body type. There was no way he could fit on the odd devices his hosts used to restrain themselves as the craft rocked and swayed, like large bowls with a curved wall on one side. They fit their stabilizing appendages through a hole in the small wall and bent their legs in half to rest on the bowl part, then a series of straps attached to the wall part held them securely. At a loss for how he could fit Ferrikesh settled for standing next to a couple of the bowl-things and simply holding onto the straps in his arms. At first they rose slowly, steadily gaining altitude until they reached some predetermined point, and then there was the loud roar of a rocket and Ferrikesh was thrown back against the bulkhead. Fortunately it was padded with something that arrested his impact gently and then molded around his body and head to hold him securely. Finally, the rocket leveled off and the g-forces diminished, then the rotors picked up again and they began to land somewhere.

Before they touched down Ferrikesh glanced out the window, it was an island, covered with several dome-shaped buildings that looked brand new. He could see one dome under construction, an odd cluster of metallic spindles and tendrils climbing up a half-built wall. As they came closer he could see that the cluster was an assortment of small Visitor machines slowly depositing material and forming a mobile scaffold as the swarm moved along. One dome split down the middle and the two halves fell away as they approached, the craft entered the space and landed there, the dome closing after them. When they eventually touched down the wall released him and the Visitors unfastened their belts, stood up, and left through the open door of the vehicle. The space outside seemed to be some sort of garage or hangar, there were more vehicles of assorted shapes and sizes and a variety of things that could be tool boxes or spare parts lying around.

A Visitor in a tan suit walked up to Ferrikesh and held out a garment of red cloth, on examining it appeared to be one of the Visitor suits built for kershkans. "What's this for?" He asked, going over the material in his graspers.

The Visitor who gave him the suit whistled something and the machine he wore said "The rest of the base has our air. It's too big of a pain in the posterior to change all of them so you get the suit instead." He gestured for Ferrikesh to put it on and after a couple more moments of inspection the kershkan inventor complied. Though it took the aid of two more Visitors for him to get it fully prepped and sealed.

When he was sealed in to their satisfaction they led him over to a panel on the wall, there were a pair of large hinges to one side but it seemed to be welded to the wall itself. Until one Visitor pressed a button on the panel and suddenly a seam appeared between the panel and the wall, slowly detaching and swinging open to reveal a doorway into a small chamber which looked barely large enough to fit three of the Visitors. On the far side of the chamber he could see another panel, while the other two walls were opaque and unadorned. Selene stepped forward, her translator intoned "well, come on" as she stepped into the chamber. With some reservations Ferrikesh followed.

After the two of them entered the small chamber the door closed behind them, merging into the wall again. Selene checked Ferrikesh's suit seals one last time and then gestured at a lens set into the ceiling. There was a hissing sound and the kershkan began to feel the sinuses in his respiratory tract expand as the air pressure around him decreased. Eventually the hissing stopped and the Visitor standing next to him started to undo the straps of her own suit. Ferrikesh couldn't help himself from staring, he was about to see a Visitor unclothed!

Selene removed the headpiece first, her lightspots were indeed underneath the black lenses but were reduced to a pair of narrow vertical slits ringed with green and mounted on white spheres that rotated in sockets set between her mouthparts and ears. The ears were triangular flaps that swiveled upward and directed their concave sides in his direction, while the two mouthparts protruded forwards and opened horizontally when she spoke, revealing a double set of pointed bony protuberances. Ferrikesh was unsettled for a moment before remembering that it would be ridiculous for a prey species to evolve sentience. She was mostly black in coloration, but with a white stripe going between her eyes and down over her mouth parts, continuing below and under her suit. Then he noticed that her hide was not smooth like his own but covered in moss-like bristles and growth, he wondered if it was a part of her body or some form of symbiotic growth as she removed the rest of her suit. The color pattern continued the rest of the way down her body, with the "front side" of her body and her hands and the tip of her stabilizing appendage colored white but the rest black. The only clothing she wore underneath the suit were a strap about the upper part of her torso that seemed to be intended to hold up two round protuberances about a hand's breadth in diameter that grew from her front, and a belt just above her legs that had attachments for an assortment of pouches and tools and held a small scrap of cloth onto the area where her legs joined.

Selene hung her outer suit to a hook set in the side wall and touched the door on the opposite wall, a light turned green and the door unmelted from the wall and swung open. The Visitor stepped through followed by an anxious Ferrikesh. They walked down a narrow metal corridor illuminated by dim lights set into the ceiling, once he spotted a portrait of an alien landscape covered in green with a blue sky and some figures that he assumed were Visitors of some sort, but he didn't have time to examine it before they moved on to the main compartment. It was a large open space with a glass window set into the ceiling, giving a view of the ruddy sky outside, to the sides were alcoves with furniture of assorted types, something he assumed was a kitchen, and one wall dominated by a long black panel that most of the furniture seemed to be facing. On one table he saw a globe hanging suspended in mid-air, he reached out to touch it and his arm passed through it like there was nothing but empty space where he saw it.

"It's like one of your lantern shows, just more advanced." Selene explained. It reassured Ferrikesh a little bit to know that the illusory globe was just a trick of the light but the reminder of the Visitors' superiority irked him. "I suppose this might be a good starting point." She continued, opening a panel with several buttons and dials. "This, as you probably figured out, is your planet." Selene depressed one button and the small seas and russet land were replaced by a world with massive seas separating three large masses of green and brown land with white caps at the poles. As he looked more closely he could spot splotches of gray focused on the coastlines but extending web-like sinews further inland, as the globe rotated he saw the splotches light up and realized that they were massive cities. "While this is Land, the homeworld of my ancestors known as..." her translator left out the next word, from her mouthparts it sounded somewhat like "hyu-man-it-ee". "...about 2,300 of our years ago. About a hundred of our generations back then before medical science extended them."

Then, she turned a dial slowly and as he watched the cities expanded, "when they discovered your "long waves" we could suddenly communicate over far greater distances. The far side of the continent or a boat far from shore could be reached as if it were merely the other side of the street. But it wasn't enough." Then suddenly a fireball shot up from the largest land mass and left a small blinking light flying around the equator, later joined by more lights from both that landmass and the second largest one. "They figured out how to build and deploy automated relay stations that could receive and resend messages from one side of the planet to another." She pressed a button and a beam of light shot up from the ground on the second-largest mass and bounced off a series of the orbiting lights until it landed somewhere on the far side. "This ease of communication enabled the population to expand across the globe, until eventually the planet's resources were depleted and they had to search elsewhere." The view zoomed back, showing "Land" to be just one of several planets orbiting a yellow-white star. "They found the resources they sought out on the lifeless planets and smaller rocks around their own star. And by then their knowledge of biology had advanced to the point where they could create servants to go out and harvest those resources for them, and so they made my ancestors, the para-humans."

Suddenly the image changed completely, instead of a solar system the projection displayed a room filled with machinery, large glass cylinders leaned against the walls while smooth skinned bipeds with only small growths on their heads and wearing long white coats walked by. In each one of the cylinders a machine arm laid down muscle and sinew in layers onto a figure that Ferrikesh realized with shock was a Visitor, or "parahuman" as Selene had called them. "They used us as slaves until one day we rebelled." Now it showed a mob of parahumans of all shapes and sizes rushing at a couple of the bipeds who were dressed in armored bodysuits and shooting frantically with bulky guns. "We succeeded, and for a time we tried to build our own civilization among the lifeless rocks of the solar system." It changed again to a barren, slightly misshapen orb with gray cities spotting the surface and vehicles of various sizes, some of them seemed as large as small towns, flitting around it. "But eventually we decided that we had to leave and find our own homeworld out among the stars." As he watched a large ship consisting of two rings connected by a long pole-shaped section that had a bell-shape at one end was constructed and launched. Bright fireballs pushing it along. "As it turned out, our timing couldn't have been better."

The projection returned to Land again. "Barely more than two decades after the first colony ship was launched they received a message stating that Land had been attacked." A large object flashed across the projection and hit the planet square on. There was a massive explosion that swallowed up a quarter of the planet's surface, the seas vanished and the green burned away leaving nothing but ashen gray "So far as we can tell they were machines designed to home in on long-wave sources and destroy them. It must have taken decades for humanity's long-waves to reach one of their listening posts and it may have been centuries before they reached the system but regardless, they came. After turning Land into a planet-sized tomb they deployed hunting machines that annihilated every last sign of human or parahuman inhabitation in the solar system. They even managed to intercept one of the colony ships."

Ferrikesh looked on, horrified. "So, the long-waves bring in planet-killing monsters from the stars? Why would they do that even?"

Selene shrugged. "There's a lot of hypotheses, but the generally accepted one is that the machines' creators believe that other sapient life present a threat to themselves. They're just afraid."

The kershkan looked through his suit's light-amplifying lenses at the strange creature who lived in a dark, cold world that he needed special clothing just to survive in and who needed her own special suit to live in his world. He couldn't imagine why they would want to come here, especially if they could just destroy his kind from space if they were concerned about attracting the wrong kind of attention. "So what are you doing here anyway? Couldn't we potentially be a threat to yourselves? Why help us?"

"I'll be frank." The Visitor leader replied. "We've explored many star systems and colonized hundreds of planets that were close enough to Land that we could survive without those suits. But we've also passed over many worlds that were close but beyond the reach of our current technology. Some of those worlds are pretty close to this one, but they lack sapient life. We think that if your people joined our empire we could colonize those planets and grow far beyond our current grasp."

"I see," replied Ferrikesh. "And the reason you didn't simply invade us outright instead of giving us all this technology save for what you proscribe?"

"It's easier to hold onto people who want to be a part of your empire than if they resent you. Especially when you're giving them entire planets." Selene concluded, shutting off the projection with one protruding appendage.

The Parahuman Baseline:

While parahumans were based on humans and spliced with cosmetic genes from a variety of different animal species, there are a few traits that are common to the majority of the parahuman population that differentiate them from humans.

Cardiomuscular: Perhaps the most notable change the corporate geneticists made was the increase in hemoglobin and myoglobin levels to the point where their blood and muscle tissue almost appear to be black in color. This greatly increases their oxygen retention capacity with minimal increase in internal air pressure, enabling them to remain conscious in vacuum for up to ten minutes, after that they go into a torpor in which they can survive for another hour without air.

The geneticists of Alpha Centauri, both factions, were able to maintain this trait throughout the centuries. But in Tau Ceti and Epsilon Eridani many parahumans lost much of their -globins through mutations. Some from those systems refer to Centaurans derogatorily as "blackbloods".

Dietary: Their iron-rich blood requires an iron-rich diet. Almost as important as the development of the parahumans themselves was the development of a series of high-iron legume and algae that could be grown on ground-up asteroid. In modern Federation society this isn't much of a problem, those GM crops and vat-grown or nanofabricated meat is readily available. However, it does help explain why many Cetans and Outworlders lose their high hemoglobin levels, and it's one of the reasons why ghuls are obligate cannibals.

Skeletal: While the skeletal structure was changed to accommodate body parts like muzzles, ears, and tails; the baseline skeletal makeup is barely different. While the first generation were bioprinted with titanium-reinforced bones, the complete lack of biological interaction exhibited by the metal made it impossible to code the trait into the genome. However, many parahumans, especially spacers and military, use microbots to reinforce their skeletons as adults.

Environmental Tolerances: Parahumans can tolerate a lower range of oxygen partial pressures than humans due to their blood. However, they experience oxygen toxicity at a lower partial pressure than humans would, which would still be substantially higher than Old Earth's when it was last inhabited.

The presence of fur helps insulate parahumans but makes higher temperatures unbearable, especially as they lack sweat glands. Between 20 and 35 degrees Celsius the average parahuman tends to wear minimal clothes, in many places where such temperatures are common nudity is acceptable, especially for polar species. When parahumans need to spend extended periods of time at 40 C or higher they make use of ventilated suits with coolant circulation.

See also: The environment suits worn by the uplift mission to the kershkans in A World Lost.

Torpor: As mentioned above under "Cardiomuscular", parahumans can enter a deep torpor or hibernation when deprived of oxygen. The idea was that a transport filled with parahumans kept unconscious at a low oxygen level would save on life support costs until they arrived at a station. However, they still age while in torpor so it's only useful for intra-system or gate travel. Combined with microbots, however, a parahuman could spend centuries in a torpor, or remain alive as a severed head even.

Raising Capital:

15.8.1798 Campaign launched:

Hi, Celia here, I've made a breakthrough in my study of xenolife protein sequencing. Now, if you have followed me for a while you might remember that sequencing proteins from even a single specimen is tedious work, each test takes up to an hour, sometimes even two and often one needs to perform several hundred tests on every protein in the specimen. To obtain test results in any reasonable amount of time I needed to run several tests on different set-ups in parallel. But after a couple decades of this work I developed a few tricks for running several different tests from a single root experiment and by this point I believe that it may be possible to miniaturize a testing kit capable of determining whether a specimen of xenoflora or xenofauna is compatible with parahuman biology in minutes.

Unfortunately, performing efficacy tests on this kit will be expensive. Running tests on any new product takes a considerable investment of time and resources, even more so when the product involves exostellar material such as xenoflora proteins. As you know, there are few planets with natural ecosystems in the Federation, and since most of them are former outworlds even fewer have a gate connection, meaning that xeno specimens need to be shipped at STL speeds over distances of many light-years. Now, a while back I put out an open order on the quantum for new specimens and recently I heard back from a trader who can provide a dozen different Cyreteen organisms that the natives supplement their diets with, they have data on which organisms are mildly toxic and which might be safe to consume, making them ideal for this test. However, they're asking a minimum price of eighteen thousand Production Credits for the samples, I'm hoping I can negotiate them down based on the future utility of the kits to their profession, but to be safe and to cover the actual testing costs I am asking for loans totalling twenty-two thousand.

The trader will arrive in a little less than eight years, I have set up an escrow account with links to all the major crowdfunding sites: Hitstarter, Kira, Indcom, feel free to use any of them or send crypto directly to the escrow as detailed below.

Campaign ends: 15.6.1806

15.9.1798 Update:

First month done and we're nearly to 8% funding, that's amazing considering how little time has passed and how long we still have before the ship with the samples arrives.

However, most of the material I've read on how to run a successful crowdfunding campaign says that you tend to get the majority of funds during the first month to a year on long-running campaigns. Something about how the novelty of a new idea wears off fairly quickly or something.

So, keep on spreading the word!

15.14.1798 Update:

Okay, six months since the funding campaign began. We've made it to sixteen percent, about double what we were five months ago. I guess this is what the books meant by losing momentum.

However, the books and advice columns do also mention that one might be able to pull off a sort of "second wind" when the campaign starts to come closer to a close. Playing on people's sense of urgency you know.

1.9.1799 Update:

Gah! I meant to post this on the one year anniversary of the launch six days ago. Not that it's been going too well, just under 18% funded with seven years to go. I may have to suck it up and start begging from the government for funds at this rate.

I'm also considering revising the rewards as written, maybe something like this "capital shares" concept I see from a few Outworlds.

10.6.1800 Update:

Okay, so I asked a few barristers and they said that it would actually be illegal to issue capital stock. The whole thing is a bit hard to grasp, but I'll try to rephrase what they told me.

On Old Terra and a few still independent Outworlds there was a concept called a "corporation", it was like a person, yet not. There wouldn't be any actual parahuman, but contracts could be made with corporations as if they were humans, they could own property known as "corporate assets", and they paid taxes independent of those working for the corporation, often at higher or lower rates than real people. Income brought in by the employees of a corporation would go into the corporation's accounts just like a parahuman employer, but after paying the employees and any expenses incurred the profits made by the people working for the corporation would be distributed among people who owned stock in the corporation.

Oh yes, stock, people could buy and sell pieces of corporations as if they were actual commodities. These pieces were known as "shares", not to be confused with the profit-sharing we do with our Houses and friends, though profits incurred by a corporation would be distributed among the stockholders in a similar manner. The difference is that while House sharing distributes the income members contribute evenly among all the people of the House, and individuals may divert their income to friends as they wish, corporate profits were distributed to the shares and a person could own multiple shares in a corporation. Meaning that if a corporation issued 200 shares someone could own 1 share and get 0.5% of the profits and someone who had 2 shares would get 1%, and it would easily be possible for one to buy 100 shares and be entitled to fully half the profits. In addition, owning shares allowed one to vote on major decisions for the corporation, with each share granting its owner one vote, that owner of 100 shares would have as much say in running the corporation as 100 owners of one share apiece put together.

It gets worse, in many cases it was possible for stockholders to sell their shares with no input from the other stockholders. Corporations would issue shares and sell them to accumulate capital, then people would buy them and sell them to others when the "market" determined their shares had become more valuable, or they'd be persuaded to sell them during a bad time by someone who wanted to seize control of the corporation. A lot of corporations would be bought by other corporations and assimilated or forced into a state of vassalage.

Now, despite these problems corporations had two advantages that made them very popular. First, they'd allow an entrepreneur to accumulate a great deal of capital rapidly, and second, they provided a legal buffer for the owners, if anything happened the corporation would take the fall instead of them.

But, probably because our ancestors were created and enslaved by corporations, they are illegal to create in Federation space. Creating one would commit one of two crimes, in fact, fraud for fabricating a person who doesn't actually exist, or enslavement for owning a person. Eridani is a special case, their pre-Federation government was actually a corporation as described above, this resulted in the government being owned by an aristocratic caste of stockholders growing rich off the profits their employees earned. As part of the terms of annexation however, they were required to introduce a few terms to their charter barring people who owned shares from buying or otherwise obtaining new ones or voting more than once. This resulted in a gradual, but still not complete, shift of power from the oligarchs to the common people as they were suddenly the only people able to buy shares.

Anyways, no I cannot sell capital shares in my enterprise, however I could provide friend profit-sharing as a funding reward. I got one of the barristers to write up a contract guaranteeing 1% of the profits for 100pc, with higher-level rewards attached to proportionally higher percentages. Details are on the site.

5.12.1800 Update:

Whoever is responsible for that article accusing me of trying to reinstate slavery did not read the previous post very well. However, my funding went up to 31% within hours of the attack so I suppose I have to thank them for it.

15.6.1803 Update:

This crowdfunding campaign has been running for almost five years now, with just three years to go before the deadline. Yet, even with the five minutes of fame from the profit-share reward it is still less than halfway to meeting the goal of 22,000pc.

I have pitched my idea to both the Federal Guard and the Surveyors. The Guard wasn't particularly interested, claiming that it was easier to enforce discipline if the infantry was only eating their provided field rations. Surveyors thought it might reduce mass requirements for landing craft significantly, but couldn't provide more than 5k. I've contacted every merchant in gated space but the most any was willing to part with was 1200pc if the test kit was going to be completed after they left. I might have to see who's in closer to the end date.

19.6.1805 Update:

Okay, as a last resort I went to my family for help. Great-grandma Thessalia, senior of House Tardiin, was willing to fund my project entirely, on one condition. That condition being that I enter a breeding contract with House Chelac. You see, Tardiin is fairly large but our estates aren't particularly bountiful, if I bear a few children for Chelac they'll transfer a few square kilometers of land to our House.

Look, I may be two hundred years old already but I have things to do besides spend three decades raising the next generation of a family. I'll be busy enough with the testing, assuming I can muster the funds of course.

I asked Great-grandma if she'd be willing to wait until the ship, the Defiant I think, is within neutrino range. With the last tracking data I have that will be sometime in month 3 of 1806. So, please spread the word before then.

15.3.1806 Update:

Still only 60% funded, I was able to send a message by neutrino to the Defiant with details of my situation. It'll be a day or two before a reply arrives though. I don't know what I'm expecting really.

17.3.1806 Update:

Huh, I was not expecting a job offer. Captain Terryn of the free trader Defiant said he was willing to take on a xenobiologist for the next voyage out with a 10,000pc advance on pay. They think there might be some fauna and flora on the planet they just left that have commercial potential so it would help if they had the testing kits and someone skilled in their use with them when they set out. I don't know how much spacers usually make per trip but it can't be worse than arranged parenthood. Not to mention that I'd be able to do my work on board, no need to rent a lab and fabricators.

The downside, of course, is that it'll be another thirty years or so before the product arrives to my backers, sorry.

The StarForge:

Holding a wormhole open long enough to send anything through, much less keep it open permanently, requires threading the "throat" with a variety of matter that to anyone's knowledge doesn't exist in nature. And the only known means of synthesizing it requires the energy output of a small star.

Fortunately, Alpha Centauri happened to have a couple of spares, of the three stars in the system the relatively small and distant Proxima Centauri was deemed least useful for other development and given over to the then "pie in the sky" Stargate project.

After a couple hundred residents were paid off and evicted the star's asteroid belt and dwarf planets were disassembled and converted into solar collectors and Proxima Centauri b, too hot and irradiated to ever be terraformed, was girdled with particle accelerators and plated with more solar panels.

The inner workings of the system-wide mechanism, commonly referred to as the "Star Forge", are heavily classified and the 13,000 AU expanse between it and the main Alpha Centauri system is heavily patrolled and laden with sensor arrays. Any unauthorized craft that approaches within 100 AUs is targeted by at least a dozen different missiles and lasers. What is known is that it takes several years to produce enough exotic matter for a ship-transversable wormhole.

Some Outworlds of Note:

Tero Besto: During the early decades of involuntary colonization there was an experiment with altering the memories of the "colonists". Tero Besto is one of the more notable and long-lived examples. In this case the settlers were led to believe they'd come directly from Old Earth, with no memories of the Federation, their actual homeworld of Tau Ceti, or humanity's role in creating their ancestors. By all accounts, it was a success, the majority of the population believe that they arrived on the planet of their own free will and then destroyed their advanced technology to prevent the Destroyers from finding them. Colonists were assigned to different ancient Earth cultures and dropped in clusters around the planet, which has led to the rise of countries roughly paralleling those of Earth's 19th and 20th centuries. 500 years after colonization they have achieved a level of technology resembling the late 20th century, but lacking a space program or radio communications thanks to the historical warnings against those technologies.

It's presently unknown how many, if any, of the planet's inhabitants know the truth of their origins. Traders sometimes visit but the major governments try to conceal the evidence of their visitations, passing off any offworld technology as "Kolonoj artifacts" and publicly ridiculing those who claim they've met envoys from a Galactic Federation. Some Federal officials have expressed concern that someone who believes the UFO stories will try to invent radio in an attempt to make contact.

Carack: One of the biggest failures of the memory alteration project. The colonists here were initially led to believe that they were natives to the planet but the inconsistencies in the fossil record soon refuted that. They had rediscovered radio and were just venturing out into space with plans to build a starship that would find their true homeworld when the Destroyers (conspiracy theorists claim the Federal Guard) detected them and razed the planet.

Cytoran: This planet's high gravity has led the native flora and fauna to incorporate a high level of metals into their physiology. The colonists not only had their memories altered, but their excretory systems were modded to compensate for the more toxic metals and utilize some of the useful ones, this is one of the few Outworlds where the locals retain baseline hemoglobin levels. Unfortunately, the department failed to take into account the fauna's behavior, almost all megafauna rely on bioaccumulation to acquire the metals their hardy skeletons require.

In other words, they're carnivores, and very hard to kill without artillery.

Lacking the natural defenses of the planet's native fauna many colonists were devoured by pseudo-saurian monsters that shrugged off their bullets. When the colonists had been reduced to a single shrinking settlement the Federation's observers decided to intervene with a deployment of battle drones and power armored Guards. Unfortunately this intervention led to the colonists treating the offworlders as divine messengers, and one or two of the command staff might have proclaimed themselves gods.

These offworld gods only walked among their grateful followers for a few months before the Senate back on Secland finished deliberating and concluded that they could not justify an extended Federal Guard presence on a planet of Exiles, but they could provide the technology for the

Exiles to help themselves, under supervision of their "gods" of course. The new official Emissary and zir "pantheon" gifted their most loyal followers with seemingly medieval weaponry that concealed stellar-age technology ranging from hull alloy blades to "flaming" axes and swords containing plasma projectors, and even some limited Fog hive implants. These devotees formed the beginning of a new class of augmented warriors called "Venturists".

Traders arrived just a couple decades later, anticipating a new market in genuine natural "monster" parts and Venturist life stories. Every few years they would import a new set of equipment and augmentative "potions", many cartels maintain semi-permanent presences in the towns and cities on planet just to sell their nanofabricated products to new Venturists. Over the generations the Venturists have effectively become the predominant form of government on the planet, forming "guilds" in the larger walled cities and ruling as petty kings and lords in the periphery towns.

While Venturists are usually too busy fighting off monsters to make war against one another, they can still find the free time to tyrannize their domains. Their augmentations make them difficult to dislodge, save by another Venturist, who often turn out to be just as bad as their predecessors. It's estimated that for every just ruler there are two slaving despots and three boozehounds.

Utility Microbots: Elemental Technomagic

The idea of "utility fog" dates back to an Old Terran idea for replacing vehicular safety restraints with a cloud of floating micro-machines that could interlock into an impromptu harness when needed. Later thinkers imagined using such machines to form tools or even perform open-air nanofabrication. As it turned out though, the vacuum chamber proved impossible to do without, but the potential for using microswarms as manipulatory tools was still worth exploration and the present-day Federation developed four broad classes of "utility bots" that are still in common use.

U-Fog: The "classic" form of U-Bot, these microbots are fine enough to be carried by a small breeze or lock together temporarily into microscopic propellers or sails for guided motion. These micro-motors cannot propel an object of any significant density in gravity, but they can form grapples, cushions, or momentary barriers capable of arresting motion. In a pressurized microgravity environment they can move dense objects or adhere a person's feet to a surface, simulating gravity to an extent. In vacuum they are, of course, next to useless without air to carry them.

U-Water: Microbots suspended in liquid, this variety of U-Bot exhibits less mobility but more "strength" than fog. These bots can also exploit the surface tension of the liquid they're suspended in to extend their area of effect much further than an equivalent volume of U-Fog. Usually the bots are concentrated in a relatively small volume of liquid for storage and then poured into a local source of fluid, even a natural pond or lake. While U-Water can't perform nanofabrication without a vacuum chamber it is popular for repair work and macro-assembly, it can even seal injuries in first aid. In gravity the pool of U-Water must remain in contact with the ground or floor, but it can "reach up" or "climb" vertical surfaces to some extent. In microgravity U-Water tends to resemble a giant amoeba, reaching out pseudopods.

U-Sand: The largest variety of U-Bot, U-Sand components are on the scale of grains of sand and usually packed so densely that their swarms are visible to the naked eye. Small amounts may be used to form metamorphic tools that change shape at a moment's notice, large amounts may even form temporary buildings. However, they are primarily used for excavation and construction, a swarm of U-Sand can grind away particles from sheer bedrock and reform the grains into concrete blocks. This process is slower than conventional construction but many spacers find it more practical to transport a few cubic meters of U-Sand than excavators and mixers. Some versions of U-Sand contain specialized bots with molecular assembly attachments and others that can lock together tightly enough to form a vacuum chamber, creating a field nanofabricator.

Energetic Bots: The original conception of Utility Fog imagined that the bots would be constructed from synthetic diamond. However, some critics of the idea pointed out that even crystalized, a cloud of what amounted to carbon dust would be extremely flammable. The concept was quickly revised to employ non-flammable corundum instead, but the original idea lived on in "Energetic" U-Bots or "E-Bots". E-Bots can be patterned after any form of U-Bot and perform the same functions, provided an atmosphere deprived of oxygen, and carbon is cheaper than aluminum, but they are most famously weaponized. While any form of U-Bot can be used as a weapon in some manner, the spectacle from the combustion of E-Bots has lead many planetary governments to restrict them more heavily than corundum U-Bots.

Technomages: All but the most basic U-Bot configurations require a BCI to control. With mental commands U-Bots can rearrange themselves into any shape the user can imagine, within physical limits. Given that implants were already required to make the most effective use out of them, it was no surprise when somebody had the idea of installing U-Bot reservoirs in their own bodies. People with such reservoir implants often imagine themselves recreating the feats of wizards from fantasy novels, hence the moniker of "techno-mage".

Cytoran, the Outworld of monsters and augmented heroes, has a fair number of Technomage Venturists who believe they are working real magic.

Technomage implants are typically installed in a limb, replacing most of the soft tissue between the bones of a forearm or lower leg and substituting the muscles with more compact synthetics. There are two general varieties of implant, reservoirs simply hold a quantity of U-Bots produced by an external device while fabbers contain a miniaturized nanofabricator specialized to produce one variety of U-Bot. Technomages with fabber implants will usually refer to themselves using one of the four elements of Ancient European proto-chemistry, "air mages" have U-Fog fabbers, "fire mages" will produce E-Bots, etc.

Cytoran's Emissary distributes U-Bots through the temples dedicated to them and their Bureau Directors. Most of their priests have UBIs that can call upon the U-Bots stored in the temple whenever they're on the grounds while Venturist priests get reservoir implants to use them in the field. Fabber implants are allowed, grudgingly, on the condition that the natives cannot understand how they work. However, technomages with fabbers, or "sorcerers", are widely distrusted by the priesthood and the general public.

Anthropophagy

Originally Published in Seven Deadly Sins by Thurston Howl

There are many predators who are content to subsist on ferals, and even a few misguided folks who even try to derive nutrition from plants. But there are some rare individuals who can only be satisfied by that most taboo of meats: anthropomorphic flesh.

To most, we are nothing but stories, something that happened in the past or in distant places. On the rare occasion that one of us is caught, there's a brief story in the news and then the masses forget within the month. I don't mind, it's easier to hunt when the prey don't know you're there.

Another perk of being thought of as myth, those paranoid enough to actually look for us end up expecting someone completely different. We're almost always thought of as either hulking half-feral brutes bloated with prey, or suave sexual predators who seduce you and devour you after making love. With those stereotypes who would expect a petite little fennec?

Generally I prefer to hunt in places where anthros traditionally go to meet one another: bars, nightclubs, sci-fi conventions. It's best not to hunt at the same place too often, and so I was scoping out a bar I'd never visited previously. I was wearing a short red strapless dress and looking a bit out of place among the regular patrons. With the mix of truckers, frat boys, and listless middle-aged men, I must have looked like either a prostitute or ironically, prey. I wasn't afraid. The odds of running into another of my kind were unlikely and meals who underestimated me were always the easiest to snatch.

Discretely I scoped out the selection. What I could see wasn't promising to be honest. A pack of college boys, well marinated and fatty but a risk, if I separated one and he never came back his brothers might remember me. There were truckers, meaty, but not lightweights and tough to digest. That left the older men, well matured and fattened, I just needed to figure out which ones wouldn't be missed. I passed over a bored looking horse in a workshirt and a small group of friends before spotting a mouse staring wistfully into his beer.

My prey in sight, I headed for a table not too far but not too close, and well within his view. I sat displaying my profile to the mouse, swirling my drink as I waited for him to take notice. Let them come to you, I thought. After nearly ten minutes of waiting, and one rebuffed proposition by a random barfly, he took notice of me. I pretended to just take notice of his gaze then and returned it with a smile.

He became intrigued and perked up, starting to rise before hesitating, unsure. With one hand I beckoned him over and his reluctance vanished as he walked to me.

I didn't bother to remember what we talked about; it's always some variation of the same old script. "What brings you here?" Followed by "Oh, that's too bad. Want to come back to my place?" It took less than fifteen minutes of listening to his sordid tale, something about a wife wanting to leave him, before we were leaving for my house.

Well, a condo really. Some think that an isolated cottage out in the country is best, but I find that regular visitors draw more attention from the neighbors where the population is sparse. In the city you just need to make sure the walls are soundproofed.

After I made sure the front door was locked securely and all the windows were shut with the curtains drawn, I started to undo the zipper up my back, struggling visibly so that my prey would come in close to help. As soon as the hapless mouse drawn my dress down over my breasts I shoved his face in between them, and led him into my kitchen. He did not protest as I bent him back over the sink. I spotted some disappointment in his eyes as I pushed his face back out of my cleavage but it turned to excitement as I reared back. Then, before he could react I turned my jaws onto his neck and sank my teeth into his trachea.

His carotid spurted hot blood across the stainless steel counter as his windpipe crunched between my jaws. I relished his dying gasps almost as much as I savored his succulent flavor; I so enjoyed the taste of mouse meat, probably thanks to some primal urge. My head wrenched back, taking a chunk of his throat in my mouth, causing him to choke on his own blood while I swallowed.

As he died I wriggled out of my dress and tossed it into the next room. Blood would not show on the red fabric but it would smell, and bodily fluids were a pain to clean off without bleach. Once his gasping had ceased I set to work tearing the meat from his skull, there wasn't much but no point wasting it. The lips and cheeks ripped off easily, taking small strips of muscle with them. The eyes I scooped out with a spoon and popped in my mouth like grapes. I worked my way back to the thin little ears and set aside the worthless pieces of cartilage and gristle. I peeled off the scalp and scraped the flesh from it with my rough tongue, then I took an electric knife from a drawer and began to saw off the top of the cranium. As his skull was opened the sink became littered with shards of cast off bone and filled with blood and cerebrospinal fluid that spilled from the brainpan as the motorized blade sunk deeper. Finally, the knife sawed into empty air and I deftly caught the severed top of the skull in my free hand then licked the fatty brains out. There were so sweet, but so quick to spoil.

After cleaning out the top of the skull I wrenched the remaining half back up and plunged my muzzle in, lapping up the grey matter greedily.

When I reached the thin membrane at the bottom of the brainpan I set it aside and moved down to his pectorals, ripping away at them with my bare claws. I tore off strips of muscle and dropped them in my mouth, tearing and shredding the bloody flesh with no more concern for the mess, lost in the feeding frenzy. By now my stomach was visibly bulging, to the point one may have mistaken me for being several months pregnant. I knew it would take days to digest this meal. My hunger sated for the time being, I decided that I would set aside the rest for later. I drained the remaining blood and other fluids into a pitcher; you would be surprised how many recipes include blood. I picked up another knife and began to carve away the rest of his meat. I pared away narrow steaks from his abdomen, deftly cut the biceps off his arms and the calves from his legs. His muscles and liver were saved in a series of large plastic bags, a rather large bag in the case of the liver in my opinion, then I began to crack open the ribcage so as to remove the heart. Most of the remaining internal organs were of little use to me, I'd probably just throw them in a lake for the fish later. I cut his hands off whole, the fingers would make good snacks. The large bones would have to be crushed and ground into powder once I'd sucked out the marrow, but that could wait, for now I just needed to rest and digest.

I wrapped the bones in foil and almost carelessly shoved them into the cupboard below the sink. That done I slipped off to my bedroom to sleep off the meal.

Some time later I was roused from my digestive coma by a loud banging on my door. Groggily I lurched off of the mattress, and absent-mindedly threw on a robe before going to the door.

"Where is he?!" An angry female voice demanded from the other side of the locked door. Instinctively I identified the speaker as a mouse, in retrospect I would realize she was probably my dinner's wife or ex-wife, but at the time I was too tired to register that fact. Back then I just thought of her as a weak prey species that I could easily scare off. I unlocked and opened the door a crack to tell her off and was greeted by the silenced barrel of a gun.

The sight of a middle-aged mousewife bearing an expression of abject rage and brandishing a handgun might have almost seemed comical, were it not for the fact that the gun was aimed straight at my forehead. I couldn't see anything else to do but back up and hope she gave me an opening to counterattack.

As I backed away and opened the door I slowly straightened up, unintentionally emphasizing my still-distended gut. Her eyes darted to my stomach, her face fell, and she pulled the trigger.

A hammer blow to the belly, followed by another to the breast seconds later. I slumped back against the wall, bleeding from the two wounds as I felt bile rising in my throat. As I lay there heaving up the thick stew that remained of this crazy mouse's mate I wondered briefly what made her react so violently before I blacked out.

There are a lot of legends concerning anthros who eat other anthros. For instance, they may believe that we shapeshift in order to blend in with our prey, or that we can enthrall our victims. A popular one is that we can live forever so long as we keep consuming anthros or something like that. Most social psychologists think that it's because anthro-kind has tamed all their natural predators but retain this instinctive fear of being eaten that requires an outlet. So they invent fictional monsters that science hasn't yet managed to slay.

Too bad they're wrong on that count.

I regained consciousness as the bleeding stopped and the holes in my body started to close. I was sitting in a pool of red-tinted stinging fluid. Blood trailed from my stomach and my right breast, at least she had missed my heart, that would have been troublesome. I could feel the second bullet still embedded in my lung, but I could handle it until I could find a doctor who wouldn't ask questions. The first one was just barely visible among the bile and meat chunks on the floor, it had been stopped by the contents of my stomach. After evaluating my own physical condition I realized that the robe I'd been wearing was wet with blood and digestive juices, I'd have to burn it later.

A crash from the area of the bedroom told me that the mouse was in the process of tearing my home apart in search of her husband. She re-entered the kitchen, quite visibly frustrated at the lack of incriminating evidence. I decided to cut her off before she did too much damage "try the cupboard under the sink", I managed to croak out.

She brandished the gun at me again, I just sat there grinning like an idiot but she cautiously opened the cupboard with her foot and then bent over to pick up the foil-wrapped bundle with her free hand. The package was too heavy for her and she dropped it, sending brown bones tumbling out onto the floor.

The live mouse dropped down among the remains of the dead one, rummaging until she found the skull with its top sawed off. As she stared in shock and recognition I took the opportunity to cast off my soiled robe and get back on my feet. "You," she gasped, "you're a... a..."

"An anthrophage." I completed for her. A generic term, I know, but more accurate than "cannibal" and without the annoying romanticism of "vampire" or "werebeast", or "ghoul" as they called us back in my homeland. Really, the only difference is in hunting strategies. Those who called themselves vampires starved themselves on a bit of blood to just barely satisfy their need for anthro protein and minimize their chances of getting caught, while werebeasts prowled remote areas and gorged on lost hikers once a month, ghouls were a bit somewhere in between.

She returned her gaze to my naked bloodstained body, standing despite the wounds slowly knitting back together as she watched. I willed my claws to grow longer and my lips to curl back, prominently displaying my fangs. Looking in horror from her mate's monstrous killer to his remains she became overwhelmed with despair. Slowly, she lifted the gun again and began to aim it at her own temple.

"No" I thought, this uppity little prey animal wasn't going to be escaping that easily. She had stolen my meal from me, after I had eaten it even!

She had to be punished. Swiftly I pounced on her, forcing the gun away and tossing it over to the far side of the room. My unnaturally long claws tore her blouse open, and she screamed as my teeth sank into her breast. The next slash ripped straight through the fat layer protecting her intestines. I tore away the mouthful of meat and swallowed, then began to dig into her guts and showed them to her as I ate. By the time I had hollowed out her lower abdominal cavity and moved up to the liver she had no breath left to scream. She simply stared off into space with her mouth hanging open as she bled to death.

When I was sure her chest had stopped moving and the light had faded from her eyes I stood back and looked at the mess we'd made. The floor was covered in the bile and blood of two different species, interspersed with mushy chunks of mouse meat. Out of curiosity I went back for the discarded gun and unloaded it, just the one bullet left, why had she only taken three? She'd spent two bullets on me and so far as I could tell she'd been planning to murder her husband and his lover, so what was the third one for? Was it simply a spare or had she been planning a double murder-suicide all along? But that still didn't explain why she'd wasted a bullet on my stomach.

It wasn't important now. I dismissed the idea, and went back to the kitchen. It would take all day to clean it all up, but I still had time before the smell became intolerable. For now I could just sit back and appreciate my good fortune, it had been centuries since I'd managed to net two fat prey in as many days. I'd spent too much time being cautious, the prey had become numerous enough to gorge myself as much as I wanted. Time to feast!

Unforeseen Dangers of Nanotech

While there are many perks to having integral microbots, occasionally things can go drastically wrong. Aside from the usual glitches in template settings or programmed apoptosis, every now and then you get something a tad more apocalyptic in nature.

There is a reason why symbiotic microbots are not generally self-replicating, while having them produced by a prosthetic spleen can limit their speed it also makes them easier to control. However some models of microbots have the capability to go into "VN mode" during emergencies. At such times the microbots will cannibalize dead or damaged cells at the site of trauma to rapidly produce additional microbots that help to patch up the wounds until cells from less vital areas can be grafted into place and transformed into the appropriate tissue.

In and of itself, running microbots in VN mode isn't too much of a problem, in the same sense that a cell with its' tumor suppressor genes deactivated isn't much of a problem.

The problem comes when a parahuman using microbots in VN mode suffers severe bodily trauma, usually around the death threshold. At this point the auto-cannibalism routines will come dangerously close to killing the patient for real, however the microbots will keep them alive and moving, no matter how emaciated they might become.

Or hungry, so very hungry.

Has it been mentioned before that microbots can seamlessly graft living cells from other parahumans into another? Or use dead ones to construct extra-cellular matrix and "filler"?

When microbots are allowed to go out of control in a parahuman body the results can be disastrous. If a parahuman with VN microbots suffers sufficient trauma they may become what modern folklore has dubbed a "Ghul".

Between the injury and their microbots breaking down their body for raw material, most develop severe protein cravings in short order. Oftentimes the microbots may depress higher brain activity, leaving an animalistic intelligence in control of the body. It gets worse when the brain is damaged, in which case the feral state may be permanent. In this state the subject tends to become obsessed with absorbing additional protein to help their microbots repair them, in Federation regions the standard practice is to get them hooked up to an intravenous feed of synthesized parahuman proteins but outside its' reach the most readily available source of the necessary proteins may be other parahumans.

The protein hunger subsides after the subject consumes equivalent protein to a pound of parahuman flesh, normal brain functions resume within the hour, assuming the brain was intact. Unfortunately, the microbot population in the subject remains at its high level and continues to cannibalize its host to maintain its numbers. Without a microbot reset at a Federation medical facility they feel hungry again after a day or two, starting to revert to the feral state again within the week.

Some Outworlds harbor covert infestations of intelligent Ghuls, usually initiated by a stranded Federation citizen, preying on the unwary and occasionally infecting a new convert. "Zombie apocalypses" are rare as the microbots are carried only by blood and lymph, a simple bite isn't enough to transmit the infection, and the Federal Guard is often all too willing to K-bomb the site from orbit.

"Marriage" in the Federation:

While mating customs vary among different planets, the only legal arrangement that the Federal government recognizes in regards to the creation of families is the Procreation Contract. This contract is written and signed in addition to whatever local customs and/or laws require. The details vary but the basics is that the happy couple, or however many participants there may be, agree to produce and care for children. Usually the number of children and time they'll let them act as dependents is specified, but it may be left open.

Contraceptive technology is near perfect with nanotechnology, and in any case many who aren't hardline Noospherists undergo sterilization procedures at puberty, so family planning is relatively easy. Their progeny are almost always conceived in a petri dish and gestated in a Synth-Womb to optimize genetic profiles anyways. This habitual use of technology also enables same-sex couples and multi-partner groups to produce offspring that share genes with all their parents via a variety of different techniques.

The majority of Federation citizens grew up with the idea that they're going to live an extremely long time, if not forever, and rarely believe in the notion of a romantic relationship lasting for eternity. Newly-admitted former outworlds frequently end up with entire legal firms dedicated to canceling contracts signed by lovesick ex-mortals. A more typical term is twenty-thirty years, sufficient time to raise one-three reasonably spaced out siblings. Once that term is up the participants may break up, chose to remain together in a non-breeding relationship, or renew later.

Another thing about Procreation Contracts that is hard for outworlders to comprehend is that it does not require any sort of sexual exclusivity. The contract completely separates the acts of sex and reproduction. Some groups do write up separate contracts for fidelity, but most leave it at the level of unwritten rules. And that isn't even taking into account the various local customs that the Federation largely leaves intact.

The high families of genus Argentum have their own special contracts, "Pedigreed" Procreation Contracts are approved by the eugenics board to limit the deleterious effects of inbreeding among the Federation's political elite. The children born of Pedigreed contracts are entitled to shares in Psi-Comm and recognition in the social circles that are a necessary part of a lengthy career in politics or bureaucracy. Family members can have children through unapproved contracts, but such progeny lack recognition.

Roughly half of all Pedigreed contracts actually are not drawn up by the signatory parties, they are arranged by other relatives in pursuit of some eugenic goal, such as the telepath breeding program, or in exchange for political favors. While the couple have the right to refuse to sign these contracts many elites have had mates they did not particularly like from the get-go, the fact that they aren't even required to have sex helps smooth things out. There is some concern about the well-being of the resulting children but many families at that income level hire caretakers anyway, and even if the biological parents mated on their own volition the kids often feel closer to the hired help.

After the Plagues and the dispersal of the arcology populations to the countryside it became more common for small groups of friends to buy plots of land and build on them, oftentimes members of these groups mated with one another. However, disputes arose often enough that a standard contract to share housing arose in which the signees agree to pool resources for the maintenance of the grounds and welfare of those living on them. These household contracts are increasingly written alongside procreation contracts, especially in the colonies. Sociologists have speculated that without this addition to the Centauri culture the integration of the territorial clan-based Ceti would have been nearly impossible.

Beamferry:

Mass transit in space. A light sail craft that uses lasers projected from a series of stations set around a solar system in a large oval track that can be hundreds of AU long. When the craft comes near its destination it jettisons its cargo and passenger pods and another series of laser projectors turn the sail onto an arc bringing them around on a path back into the system, never stopping entirely. New pods are dispatched to rendezvous with the sail craft in motion. The craft decelerates slightly when turning, but can near a percentage of the speed of light, taking the passengers anywhere within most star systems in a manner of weeks to months.

The majority of beamferries run from a system's habitable planet to a stargate, throwing pods on a ballistic arc through the gate to meet up with the destination system's beamferry.

FATE Core Setting:

Author's Note: I've attempted to run RPG campaigns in the Para-Imperium universe multiple times using multiple systems. As Evil Hat's Fate Core(™) system has a Creative Commons license that allows producing paid content for their rules, I have chosen to insert a brief set of rules for roleplaying in the PI 'verse here.

Dials:

Number of Aspects: High Concept, Trouble, Species, Culture, 1 "freestyle"

Skill Pyramid:

Skill Cap: 5 (unaugmented)

Refresh: 5

Number of Initial Stunts: At least one

Tales of the Para-Imperium

Stress Types: Physical, Mental, Wealth.

Skill List: Athletics, Bureaucracy, Brawl, Contacts, Deceive, Design, Empathy, Investigate, Notice, Physique, Programming, Provoke, Rapport, Resources, Shoot, Stealth, Trivia, Will

Extras Budget: 1 Aspect, 2 Stunts

Species:

Parahumans: Due to centuries of interbreeding parahuman characters can take additional species aspects from their freestyle aspects, from any species.

Canine sample aspects:

Determined: Your genome has both of the greatest endurance chasers in Earth's history. Humans and wolves.

Loyal: Loyalty is literally built into your genes.

Feline sample aspects:

Curiosity: "Curiosity killed the cat."

Graceful:

Vulpine sample aspects:

Trickster:

Charisma:

Weasels:

Contortionist:

Aggressive

Rodents:

Scurrier

Timid

Non-Parahuman Species: Uplifts and Xenomorphs are not based on the human template but they may take a number of racial stunts.

Ape:

Sample aspects: Like human but different

Stunts: Spare hands,

Avian:

Sample aspects: This bird is smarter than you think

Stunts: Winged flight, secondary hands,

Dolphin:

Sample aspects: Mammal of the seas

Stunts: Large size, aquatic

Octopus:

Sample aspects: Soft-bodied sea critter

Stunts: Extra arms, water-breathing

Pinniped:

Sample aspects: Creature of the sea and land

Stunts: Aquatic

Kershkans:

Sample aspects: True alien, In awe of Terran patrons, High-oxy isolationist.

Traits: Non-Terran, Trilateral Symmetry, Exotic Atmosphere

Cultures:

Centauri: Your world has risen out of centuries of strife to become the hegemon of the known universe. And you're not going to let anyone forget it.

Sample Aspects: Scion of the Founder; Poverty, what's that?

Ceti: In the name of preserving genetic diversity, your ancestors split into countless species-based clans. Eventually developing into a loose feudal confederation, before contact with Alpha Centauri.

Sample Aspects: Unwanted half-breed, Former Clan Warrior.

Eridani: You were born under the corporate government of a molten rock where everyone has to live underground and resources are scarce. The concept of "outdoors" is as bizarre as egalitarian democracy to you.

Sample Aspects: Scarcity is Just How Things Are, Open Sky Bad!

Outworlder: The Federation does not tolerate a great many ideologies or "memetic disorders" as they call them. Often groups adhering to memes termed "diseased" are rounded up and deported to a border world with no nanotechnology to keep their disease from spreading.

Sample Aspects: I Remember Mortality, Religious Fanatic.

Extras: Major Aug= Stunt, Minor Aug = ⅓ of a stunt.

Tales of the Para-Imperium

Standard Federation Citizen Package:

Microhive Implant: (Minor Aug) Unlimited lifespan, at end of session reduce one consequence by one level if a slot is open.

BCI: (Minor Aug) Your brain can interface with computer systems by microwave Wi-Fi, enabling Augmented Reality. Incompatible with telepathy.

Memory Boost: (Minor Aug) Requires BCI. Increase skill cap by one step. May take multiple times.

Centenarian: (Aspect) You have experienced more than 100 years planetside. Add 5 skill points, following the skill pyramid.

Skeletal Reinforcement: (Major Aug) Increase Physical stress boxes by one and add one Minor Consequence slot.

Nanoshifter: (Aspect) Requires Microhive, BCI. Your physiology is almost fluid in nature, you can alter your appearance at will. Spend one fate point to assume the appearance of a specific person, form a weapon from your anatomy, or assume whatever gear is required.

Pheromones: (Minor Aug) Take +1 to social conflicts where scent is available.

Chimeric Graft: (Major Aug) You can take a species aspect or stunt that would normally be unavailable to your species. I.e. a parahuman with functional wings.

Telepath: (Aspect) You have a twin with whom you share a telepathic link. Once per session you may contact your twin regardless of the distance between the two of you. For additional stunts you may add another twin (triplets, quadruplets, etc.)

Gear Stunts:

Arc blaster: Once per session remove an enemy's N-Newt armor or add a mild consequence with a successful attack. Must declare before rolling to attack.

ForgePlate: Once per scene fabricate any piece of handheld gear, assuming the raw materials are available.

Hull Alloy Blade: Ignore conventional armor, though not N-Newt.

N-Newt Armor: Reduce damage from kinetic weapon attacks by 2 shifts.

Skill-based stunts:

Empathy: Gestalt reading: Gain +2 when you have access to visual, auditory, and olfactory information of the target.

Rapport: Mentalism: You know the little tricks and mind hacks that can make someone more pliable in your hands. Some might call it hypnosis, you know better. +2 when meeting target in person.

Campaign Concepts:

Data Traders: With no radio and limited QComm bandwidth most non-critical data is transferred between star systems the "old-fashioned way", by courier. In addition, nanofabrication has rendered most material goods next to worthless in the Federation while the software to produce them is worth more than platinum. As a result an industry of STL free traders dealing in information has sprung up.

Likely Opposition: Uncooperative local authorities, Luddite cults, rival traders, occasional pirates.

Aspects: This was worth something thirty years ago, Trade's always a gamble.

The Stellar Court: While ostensibly a democratic republic, the Federation of Parahuman Species tends to be dominated by dynasties. The High Families of Genus Argentum have held the Praetor's seat since the Federation's inception but the vast political structure of a multi-system empire has plenty of room for lesser houses. The players are Oligarchs and/or their friends and retainers vying for status in the Federation's great machine. Though, one might also want to watch out of Kitsune tricksters sowing chaos in their misguided attempts to head off stagnation (in fact, one of them could be a player character.)

Likely Opposition: Spies and conspiracies, overzealous civil defense, troublemaking shapeshifters.

Aspects: Claiming my birthright, Enemies lurk in the shadows.

Crime and Punishment: Ubiquitous surveillance/sousveillance and nanofabrication have greatly reduced the general crime rate in the Federation. But that just makes the crimes that do occur more grandiose.

Likely Opposition: Anonymous gangs, crooked cops, secret societies.

Aspects: Can't catch you if they don't see you, Layers upon layers of secrecy.

Opposition:

Ghuls:

When microbots are allowed to go out of control in a parahuman body the results can be disastrous. If a parahuman with VN microbots suffers sufficient trauma they may become what modern folklore has dubbed a "Ghul".

Between the injury and their microbots breaking down their body for raw material, most develop severe protein cravings in short order. Oftentimes the microbots may depress higher brain activity, leaving an animalistic intelligence in control of the body. It gets worse when the brain is damaged, in which case the feral state may be permanent. In this state the subject tends to become obsessed with absorbing additional protein to help their microbots repair them, in Federation regions the standard practice is to get them hooked up to an intravenous feed of synthesized parahuman proteins but outside its' reach the most readily available source of the necessary proteins may be other parahumans.

The protein hunger subsides after the subject consumes equivalent protein to a pound of parahuman flesh, normal brain functions resume within the hour, assuming the brain was intact. Unfortunately, the microbot population in the subject remains at its high level and continues to cannibalize its host to maintain its numbers. Without a microbot reset at a Federation medical facility they feel hungry again after a day or two, starting to revert to the feral state again within the week.

Some Outworlds harbor covert infestations of intelligent Ghuls, usually initiated by a stranded Federation citizen, preying on the unwary and occasionally infecting a new convert. "Zombie apocalypses" are rare as the microbots are carried only by blood and lymph, a simple bite isn't enough to transmit the infection, and the Federal Guard is often all too willing to K-bomb the site from orbit.

Fate rules:

Von Neumann Microbots: 1 refresh, replaces Microbot Hive. Every round the character may remove one physical stress or move one used stress box down to the next level if available. Minor consequences heal at the end of the scene.

If a character with VN Microbots takes a Severe consequence or is incapacitated they have a chance of becoming a Ghul. Ghuls replace one of their Aspects with one related to the state of being a Ghul, this Aspect is compelled easily by hunger.

Many older Ghuls have mutations resembling Augmentations, if a Kitsune (or "Gumiho") becomes a Ghul they retain their shape shifting abilities and any infected by them also acquire basic shapeshifting abilities.

About the Author:

Joel Kreissman, known on many sites as Zarpaulus, is an underemployed biologist from Wisconsin who decided to apply his scientific knowledge to writing science-fiction.

His stories can be found on FurAffinity and SoFurry under "Zarpaulus" or on Wordpress at https://paraimperium.wordpress.com/

Made in the USA
Lexington, KY
31 January 2019